Books by Valerie Martin

Set in Motion
Alexandra

ALEXANDRA

Alexandra

VALERIE MARTIN

FARRAR STRAUS GIROUX

New York

C. 4

Library of Congress Cataloging in Publication Data
Martin, Valerie / Alexandra / I. Title.
PZ4.M38443Al [PS3563.A7295] 813'.5'4 79-10243

For my parents

John and Valerie Metcalf

"How wonderful, how very wonderful the operations of time, and the changes of the human mind!" And following the latter train of thought she soon afterwards added: "If any one faculty of our nature may be called *more* wonderful than the rest, I do think it is memory. There seems something more speakingly incomprehensible in the powers, the failures, the inequalities of memory, than in any other of our intelligences. The memory is sometimes so retentive, so serviceable, so obedient—at others, so bewildered and so weak—and at others again, so tyrannic, so beyond control!—We are to be sure a miracle every way—but our powers of recollecting and of forgetting, do seem peculiarly past finding out."

JANE AUSTEN
Mansfield Park

ALEXANDRA

A middle-aged, single, dissatisfied
man gives up his depressing life for
a triangular relationship with two
remarkable women, a relationship
charged with both women's deep need
for him.

1

Once, when Mona scrutinized her full lips in her compact mirror, just as she was raising the lipstick to smear them with crimson, she noticed that I, too, was examining her reflection, and as she saw this, there rose, through her perfectly vain concentration, an expression of childish confusion. She slapped the mirror closed in her hand and allowed her shoulders to slump forward as she turned to me.

I remember this movement of her shoulders with regret, for I had not wished to see it, not the first time, nor on any of the successive occasions in which it has risen, against my will, to my mind's eye.

But there are images in every imagination which will continue, despite, or because of, our determined efforts to erase them. I have only to say Mona's name, "Mona," and her face appears, her cloying whining voice, her big teeth and puckering lips, and I marvel that once I lay in her arms and thought myself fortunate. Because she has been so instrumental in my present state of loss, she sits now like a devil in my imagination and I have to remind myself that she is really no more than a lonely widowed lady with perfect teeth, sharp and white.

Her dear departed one had been in temperature control; he

repaired air-conditioners and heaters, a profitable profession in this sultry climate. He was much in demand and worked harder than he should have, for one balmy spring afternoon, while sweating in a cramped and steaming attic, he stood up, cracked his head on an overhead beam, fell semiconscious onto the duct of the broken central air unit, struggled momentarily, suffered a cataclysmic heart attack, and died. He left his wife well provided, and she lamented his loss for a seemly period, after which she suffered from such extremes of uncontrolled temperature (hot flashes, cold chills) that she began to look around for his replacement. Mutual friends brought us together, certain that we would do one another good, she was so bright and cheerful and such a good cook and I was so glum, poverty-stricken, dull and thin. And we were roughly the same age.

Mona took me in hand right away, cleaned my apartment, stuffed my larder, took me out to expensive restaurants twice a month, chewed my earlobes, straddled my scrawny girth with her thick, aging, and demanding thighs, and in general did all that was necessary to reduce me to a whimpering child with cringing testicles and watery bowels. I was an easy mark; at least, it was easy to move into my life. Her difficulty came in getting me to move into hers, which I steadfastly refused to do. She waited for this concession with nerve-shattering complacency and every single week called me up to describe the culinary temptations she was preparing for me at her suburban paradise. If only I would make the easy little trip out to see her.

The thought of the bed she had shared with the temperature-control man froze my blood in its murky progress through my veins and it is to my credit, I think, that I refused her and entertained her always, as best I could, in my own poor quarters.

I say all this in retrospect, for the sad truth is that for a long time I enjoyed Mona's affections and bank account with a sense of gratitude if not wonder. I couldn't understand, no

4

matter how I tried, what it was she saw that made her so dead set on having me, and in my ignorance I thought it must be some good, some quality I didn't know I possessed. Too late and with incredulity did I learn that all she saw in me was living and available flesh.

She wanted all of me and more of me than there was. She wanted me fat and satisfied and she was selfless in her determination to have me so. It's easy for me to make light of her deep despair and my own willingness to be dragged into it, now that I am free of it and have forgotten what it was like to lie beneath the weight of it, bloated and featureless like a drowned man.

A lot of things are easier now. On one or two occasions in the last six months, I have awakened with a smile on my lips, a feeling of delicious anticipation, a shuddering in my heart, my loins, the tips of my fingers and toes, to look around my spacious and sunny room at Beaufort and alight at last on Alex's dark hair and perfect features, deep in sleep on the pillow next to mine.

But that's unusual. Although I am as happy as I think I can be, it is my habit to wake in pain. My throat aches, dry and constricted. My hands and feet are stiff with arthritis, my back aches, and it hurts to straighten my knees. My eyeballs throb. I open my eyes with trepidation, expecting to find myself in my own bed with Mona snoring volubly at my side, or—slightly worse—in some deep pit of hell where tempting water will remain always just out of my reach and eternity will devour my heart with half glimpses of Alex going around a corner, slipping past me down a burning hall, smiling sleepily at me as she reclines in the embrace of another.

Clearly I would rather talk of Alex but I dare not dispense with Mona so cavalierly. Had it not been for her appetite, her ceaseless yearning to swallow everything in sight, I would never have found Alex and lived to tell this tale.

Mona loved bars, especially after a meal. My own taste in establishments of this kind runs to darkness, quiet, the smell

5

of urine and Pine-Sol. Mona soon tired of this and I agreed to tour, at her expense, the various dens advertised in the local press. We attended discos—woefully out of place in our unstylish clothes and tired eyes, we didn't dare attempt any of the gyrations demonstrated by the young upon the dance floor. Mona would have, I think, but I made a plea for the dignity of age or some such foolishness, appealing to what would have been her sense of the absurd had she possessed one, and she gave in. Still, she tapped her fingers on the tabletop and smiled demurely into the youthful eyes that settled in shock and dismay upon her coiffure, a creation of strange coils and impregnable knots gleaming with pins and spray. Then for a while we discovered hotel bars, one after the other, where waitresses in scanty costumes enveloped us in their heady scents and sometimes the room revolved and sometimes the revolution was purely metaphoric. The patrons were more to my taste; they looked like Mona and paid no attention to her posturings, being absorbed in their own preenings and dreary flirting. Mona never liked the music in these places; it was "old-fashioned." So we tried some quiet unadvertised specials. We found them by driving around and around in the Quarter, Mona hanging from the car window and calling out her estimation of what went on behind each smoked pane and half-open door. One night, despairing of anything new, we were driving down Esplanade when Mona spotted something "interesting," and I simultaneously named and claimed something even more unusual, a legal parking place. We climbed out of Mona's sleek auto and ducked into the bar, both feeling lucky and in dangerously high spirits.

What an inexorable double stroke of fate that was. I dragged myself through the whole penny-pinching joyless tedium of my life and then, slash, all of it for nothing as I saw through the smoke of the dimly lit bar, like the sun thrusting strong rays through the grayest clouds, Alex's clear eyes and intoxicating smile. I shoved Mona's wide behind through the crowd, straight for Alex and my one big shot at eternal life. I remember every grisly detail of this, our first, encounter.

Mona's well-preserved flesh was stuffed into a black gown which threatened at every turn and crease to burst its straining seams. Her décolleté exposed not only more of her ample breasts than was necessary, but more than was desirable. She leaned all this warm bulk over the bar ("This is a young people's bar," she murmured excitedly, fishing in her purse for some I.D. as we walked in the door) and looked up and down at the wall of enticing bottles. Alex glanced at us, then looked away. "What do you want?" I asked florid Mona, who rolled her eyes up, indicating that the universe did not hold what she really wanted. She squinted at the row of bottles before her and replied at last, "A Pink Squirrel."

Stout heart that I am, I did not bat an eye. While Mona craned her neck in a circle, sizing up the patrons of the bar, I turned to watch Alex.

Alex is tall and spare and her figure makes those around her look unevolved. When I first saw her I was impressed by her long neck and straight back and her posture, which contrives to be both regal and relaxed. There is something equine about her but she is by no means a "horsy" woman. The attribute she shares with horses is not in her bones but in her philosophy. She is sudden, determined, flashy, a little skittish, but powerful, fast, and courageous. She doesn't toss her head but she does bare her teeth when she is angry or when she is excited. That first night I watched her shaking water from the glasses she then filled with liquor, her hands occupied with one task and her mind pursuing another and I thought of a racehorse I had once seen grazing in a field and of how he could not keep his wild thoughts on his meal but kept looking up, chewing abstractly and dreamy-eyed, thinking of running, always running. Alex looked into the space just over my left shoulder, her mouth slightly ajar, considering something. Then she pursed her lips, lifting her eyebrows slightly, and turned away to deliver the drinks she had un-

7

consciously prepared to the waiting customers. After a moment she returned to our vicinity and began indifferently wiping an invisible spot on the counter. I engaged her attention by pulling the end of her cleaning rag out of her hand. She gave the rag a look of consternation, then lifted her face. There were no sparks but our eyes held and I tried to say something admiring with mine. She took the rag from me, wearily folding it in a neat square, which she jammed into her back pocket, clearly bored by the offer she was about to make. "Can I help you?" she inquired.

I thought of the many ways that she could help me and could not speak. She turned to Mona, who, seized by her usual compulsion to "freshen up" every twenty minutes, was digging through her bag for mirror and lipstick. Alex looked back at me and our eyes met again, briefly, distantly. "Scotch on the rocks," I said. "And a Pink Squirrel for this lady."

An expression of intense pain knit her brow even as the corners of her mouth lifted into a smile. She turned to Mona and inquired, "What is it you want, honey?"

Mona met her gaze, courageous, contemptuous. "A Pink Squirrel."

Alex was bored. "Do you think this is the Roosevelt?" she asked.

"I beg your pardon," replied Mona, undaunted.

I couldn't bring myself to name the item a second time. "She means she doesn't know how to make one of those," I interrupted.

"Well then. A rum collins."

Alex looked from Mona to me for confirmation. "A rum collins," I repeated, trying my damndest to hold her attention. She turned away and engrossed herself in the preparation of our drinks. In a moment she set them before us and we were left to ourselves. I couldn't concentrate on Mona's chatter, though I knew it was about the meal we had just shared at the new hotel restaurant downtown. The food had been well prepared, served with solemnity and colorful trappings, the wine was, yes, I agreed, the wine might have been better. Mona was content, packed full of potatoes, veal, and bearnaise sauce, and her head swimming from the wine she had not thought quite good enough. From time to time I turned my attention to her to see how fast she was going under and how soon I would be able to whisk her back to her neat bungalow and return to devote myself to the observation of Alex.

For I knew at once that she was extraordinary and I want to point out that I wasn't mistaken. She paid no attention to me then, she was busy serving customers and for the most part she showed me her back. I saw that it was fine and straight, I couldn't see how fine then. She was wearing a white long-sleeved blouse, buttoned at the cuffs, of a silky material, luminous in the soft light, almost transparent; black pants with a thin alligator belt, flaring slightly at the knee and fitting easily over her boots. I was to become intimately acquainted with those boots but didn't know it then and couldn't see them at all well from my vantage point across the bar. As I know them now, I will stop and describe them. Plain but handsomely crafted brown leather boots; the leather is so thin and soft it feels like a peeling skin; the long tongue falls away from her shin with maddening delicacy when she props her foot up on a chair and bends over the laces, tightening them resolutely through each set of holes. There are a breathtaking fifteen pair of holes to the top and by the seventh unbidden tears stand in my eyes as I sit on the edge of one bed or the other, until she turns, laughs, and plucks from my lap (where I have been fondling it in the hope of breaking the spell that keeps me from changing into it) the mate to the fortunate one now clinging to her smooth calf.

What else did I see? Her clothes, her posture, and something more. Her open, clear, and intelligent eyes, imparting to her otherwise ordinary features an expression I have seen on no one else. There is no guile in the expression with which she confronts a world that should rightly spread itself out at her feet.

The intelligent women I'd known before her all had something desperate about them, something burning and grinding, something in their brains that made them look as if they were in pain, on fire, flaming up, smoldering, or threatening to go out altogether. I thought her, most of all, relaxed, comfortable, sure of herself without trying (or having to try) to assert herself. A friend of mine (ignorant, useless, and no longer a friend) who met her described her to me as "a little masculine, but nice." I suppose the foul-minded, when seeing her, see nothing more. But having dreamed of such a woman all my life I knew her when I saw her and she could not have been (couldn't be) more to my taste had I molded the curves of her superior clay with my own hands. I watched her.

Mona droned on and on, a big fat insect I wanted to slap. All our good times together, all the temperature-control man's hard-earned cash she had lavished upon me, all the web of gluttony and greed she had spun about me so that I hung suspended before her, a meal to anticipate, all fell away and I sat in stupefied silence. She interpreted my ennui as indigestion and with a few groans and nods I gave her to believe that this was so. I would be best off at home in my own bed, alone, I admitted sadly, and besides it was so late, after leaving her clucking self and her car at her place (she couldn't drive with all the wine clouding her judgment), I would barely make the last bus home.

Reluctantly we left that great night spot and I tucked Mona away, protesting weakly, in Metairie. I did indeed barely make that last bus back and arrived at Alex's bar at something after one. She was still there, fitting and refitting her long straight spine into a corner near the cash register, in conversation with her replacement, an Italianate young man who smiled over her shoulder as she spoke. He spotted me and indicated that he would soon be with me but Alex, moved by divine inspiration or her generous nature, came instead. Did she remember me from the Pink Squirrel incident? I couldn't tell. She took my order without comment and in a moment my drink was before me and she was turning away again. My voice became a wad of cotton in my throat but I got my lips open and a contorted sound issued forth, a sound that could have been "wait" or "what." I don't know what it was; perhaps I wanted water. She heard me, took pity on me, gave me for the first time her full attention.

"You want something?" she asked.

Here was opportunity but my brain missed crankily, tired engine that it was. I gestured with my hands, rolling one over the other, then came weaving out of it, palms up, elbows on the bar, head thrust forward so that I nearly touched her with my dry aching lips and she backed away.

"Are you okay?"

Did I disgust her? I came abruptly to myself. "That's my impression of a drunk person," I said. "Is it any good?"

She smiled a little. A little smile but I detected it; it was mine. "Very good. One of the best I've seen," she said. "You could have fooled me."

"I'm back," I said. Miraculously, here were words coming out, though I couldn't have said what they meant. "I wanted to show it to you."

"Show what to me?"

"My impression."

"What happened to your lady?"

"My Pink Squirrel?"

She laughed and my heart leaped in its bony cage. If I could amuse her a few moments longer we would be deep in conversation. And after that we would exchange names. And after that? But I had to think of something to say before her laughter faded. My head ached. I looked at my hands and noticed, to my horror—though I've seen them often enough before—the swollen joints, the creases about the knuckles, the pale blotches across the backs, the hands of a man who is even older than I am. Perhaps I have neglected to mention that, but for these traitor hands, I have the face and form of a younger man, though how much younger I can't say. Ten years possibly, ten black years I passed frozen and numb, shuffling figures at the government office. Or was it twenty? But there were my hands, shocking and shaming me so that I pulled them away, a foolish gesture that cost me my composure, and an unnecessary one, for Alex was not looking at my hands, and even if she had, in that light she wouldn't have seen the impending death I saw.

"Is something wrong?" she asked sweetly and without a trace of accusation.

"I was wondering if you could leave here. Or do you stay here always?"

She glanced over her shoulder at the clock. "I leave here in fifteen minutes," she said. "You want to go with me?"

It was so simple. Easier than falling off my barstool, which I somehow failed to do. In fifteen minutes she came out from behind the bar and I accompanied her out the door and into the street, our destination enchanting and nebulous.

On that long lonely bus ride back to town I had let my imagination off its leash and the most satisfying fantasy I had (because the most possible) was that she might say a few words to me. Now I walked down a public street at her side, unable for a block or so to speak, such was my puzzlement and deep pleasure.

She broke this happy silence. "What's your name?" she asked.

"Claude."

"I've never met a Claude before."

"I hope you won't regret it."

"Why should I?"

Why should she? Why shouldn't she? And how could she be so affable with a perfect and older stranger? I noticed, however, how neatly she failed to give me her name, though I had overheard it in the bar and didn't need to ask. She walked so quickly I had to shake my head clear to keep up with her. Gradually I understood that while our destination was a provocative mirage to me it was a dead certainty to her.

"Where are you going?" I inquired.

"I'm just going home, like I do every night."

"Where is that?"

She pointed at the thin air, then slashed it from left to right with a gleaming forefinger. "Three blocks this way, two that way."

I imagined myself in a room, a magical room she passed through every day, leaving it rich with the things she cast off, her silken blouses, her alligator belts, her calfskin boots. "You really don't mind my coming along?" I said.

She turned to look at me in the street-lamp light. "For someone whose intentions are so obvious," she said, "you sure are shy."

"I'm not shy, I'm just unsure of myself."

"You don't usually pick up women? Am I the first woman you've ever picked up?"

Certainly I had allowed myself to become the unwitting companion, walking, talking, and bedding, of women I didn't know as well as I should have, for if I had I would not have done so. But I had never been in the company of any who appraised me so candidly. "What can I say?" I said.

It was dark but I saw her nostrils inflate to accommodate a rush of air, a sniff. She sniffed at me. We turned a corner and walked briskly on. "It doesn't matter what you say, Claude," she informed me. "Because the truth is you haven't even picked me up yet."

"I'm not sure what that entails."

"What?"

"Picking you up. But I would like the opportunity . . ."

"I can see that."

"Do you think I'll ever get it?"

She thrust her hand deep into her pants pocket, fished

out a silver key, and held it up before me, teasing me. "The key?" she asked.

She turned to an iron gate. "This is the gate." She put the key into the lock. "And this is the key."

"And this I take it is goodbye?"

"For tonight, Claude," she said, turning to me, inches from me, her cool eyes on my nervous face. "What is it you want, Claude?"

"Only to be of service to you. In any way. Anything."

She considered it. "To be of service?"

"Does the idea have no appeal to you at all?"

She pressed her thumbnail against her upper teeth, such a simple gesture and one that is engraved on my heart. "I wouldn't say," she said, "that it has no appeal whatsoever."

"I'll take that as good news."

"I think you should," she said. Then she turned, opened the gate, and pushed it closed behind her without looking back and I was alone on the street without, I swear, any surety, save my determination to try that gate again.

2

An hour later I was in my own rooms. I looked with a stranger's eyes. Already I could see Alex standing in the doorway, looking at the dirty rugs and stacks of dusty books. The place was always dark, as dark as her bar, and it had the same humid smell. Would it depress her?

I couldn't deny that it depressed me. On the street I had been a man of no origins, who might well contain the soul of grace and ease that this superb young woman would find irresistible. In my apartment I came home to myself and my despair was the same dark net that swarmed over me every night like an army of black ants.

I put up my same old good fight, more from habit than from any real desire to cheer up. I didn't sit down and review my own history, but I did look around my rooms for some sign of life. There was a pile of unwashed clothing in the corner, the scrambled sheets on my bed, my books, in alphabetical stacks every two feet around the walls, the papers on my desk, the photograph of a woman pressing a violin beneath her chin, the bow poised in space before her as she looked out past it, out of her wooden frame, hesitantly, as if she could really see the place, a frail plain woman now dead, my mother. The rest of the place was an advertisement for squalor. Grime was packed into every available space, roaches reigned in the kitchen. It shocked me to see how I lived, for I fancy myself a fastidious, even discriminating person. For the most part I never looked at the place, except on the rare occasions when I brought a lady home with me and had to endure the dismay in her eyes when she saw it. I made apologies: "I've been meaning to clean this place up, I've been out of town, I've been vandalized." The foul place didn't hurt my relations with these women; on the contrary, it introduced that element of pity so essential in the seduction of certain members of their sex. When Mona stepped through the door, her matron's eyes filled with tears and as I pushed her back upon my narrow bed she looked around her, at the work cut out for her, and lay down readily with an expression of delight. That very night she checked out my poor supply of cleaning aids, one can of Ajax and a sponge, pronounced them inadequate, and made a date to return and "straighten up."

"I'll get to it," I said.

"But I would enjoy it so much. It would mean so much to me."

Mona had an insidious power. She had once been a most attractive woman, I've no doubt of that. She still pursed her lips and crossed her legs in a manner that suggested she expected action and was used to getting it. She combined these two gestures, looking around at my soiled nest, and said, "Really, you know you're going to need help with this. You can't clean and have a job, too."

For a while I let her have her way. She cleaned every two weeks, with her electric brooms and mops, her sponges, metal pads, and cleansers. Armed to the teeth, she fought the threatening crud. I soon tired of this, and spent my own money on a vacuum cleaner, some cans with lemons on them, a mop, and a bag of sponges. My cleaning was not as good as hers and she complained of it but I demanded my rights as a tenant. The result was the return of my once intimidated insect buddies, a recrudescence of mold and grease in the corners, on the baseboards, and along the sink, a faint odor of rot that reassured me. I was neither ashamed nor proud of my rooms. I looked on them as mine alone and the arguments I had with Mona about my right to keep it that way left me weak with rage while she resorted to trembling lips and liquid looks.

The memory of these arguments shamed me. I thought of Alex and knew at once, without regret, that Mona must go. It might appear that I was disproportionately sure of myself, ready to throw out an old reliable girl for an unknown quantity, and in fact I had no reason to believe Alex would ever be mine. Our conversation had been brief; she had toyed with me pleasantly enough, but mightn't she tell me to get lost forever and call the police if I pursued the game?

I thought not. First there was my age, which with an ordinary woman of Alex's age (I judged her to be thirty and was correct) would be a liability. A man her own age would desire a pliable mate to dominate or elevate, depending on his character. Faced with Alex's candor, her glittering glacial eyes, he would lose interest at once. A man of forty, an insecure nervous creature who is trying to determine whether he's a success yet, will be soon, or has it passed him by, wants from women only one commodity, the conviction of potency. Alex might prove an interesting challenge to those few who are successful and confident at that age, but what would they be doing in her bar? Perhaps her doctor had plans for her, her landlord might invite her in for drinks in the afternoon, but the manners of these men, their complacency, would put her off. I was sure of it. Only a man of my advancing age, calm and chivalrous, resolute, with nothing much to lose, would do. (The possibility of a much younger man, say twenty, or, worse, a slim-hipped boy, emerged in my calculations at this point, but I shoved him purposefully down and away.)

When I told her that my wish was to serve her (and so it

was and is still, in spite of my determination to go down and make the same offer to Diana), I flattered myself that I had said the right thing. I felt confident that if I gave her three nights to think on it and then appeared to renew my offer she would have had enough time to grasp the intriguing possibilities I offered and her response would be favorable.

But what would I do about my sad sick self? I would have to appear lighthearted when I was lead-weighted. Suppose I did get her to share her bed with me, how would she endure the sight of me, waking up with my claw hands, my aching back, my skeleton's face. And what of those nights when I am brushing death off my shoulders like dandruff and I fight the darkness, suffocating and frantic, wouldn't that sight repel her?

And how about the way I sit in my chair, wringing my hands, for all the world like a weeping child, but for the tears I no longer have the wherewithal to shed?

I used the three nights I had set aside for her consideration of my offer in speculation of this kind. But I had made my decision on that first night and none of the eventualities with which I reviled my fancy dissuaded me from my original plan. On the fourth night I was at my appointed place, strolling confidently through the door of Alex's bar.

And there she was, pale and cool. She gave me a terse smile of recognition as I propped myself against the barstool. She finished the drink she was preparing, shoved it across the bar to an overweight patron who fumbled his change back to her, then came toward me, speaking inaudibly to her co-worker as she passed. "I thought I dreamed you," she said, wiping the wet counter in front of me with her soft cleaning rag.

"And how did you feel about that dream?" I heard my reply with satisfaction.

"I thought it was a dream," she paused, folding her rag. "You know. Not real?"

I wished it were a dream. Then anything might happen.

And I might not know better than to expect anything to happen.

"Maybe it is a dream?"

She wrinkled her nose and her upper lip lifted slightly, revealing a moist nacreous line of teeth. "Boy, I haven't heard a line like that since I was in school."

"I'm sorry," I said. I was flustered. "The stuff I say is old because I'm old."

"I'm sure you can't be as old as you seem to think you are."

"How old is that."

"A thousand."

A thousand sounded about right. At that moment I thought it was the awkwardness of my position and the point-lessness of my suit, but since then I have learned that she makes me feel a thousand years old all the time. The way she leaps out of bed and pulls on her clothes, her long limbs flashing by me as I suffer the anguish of placing my feet on the floor and testing them one at a time (one morning they will not hold me up), and I am so ancient I have to cover my face so she won't see it in my eyes.

"No," I said. "I'm not that old."

"So, where've you been?"

"I thought you might not want to see me. That I had annoyed you."

"That's nice. Did I say you annoyed me?"

"Not in so many words."

"How about this. If you annoy me, I'll tell you."

"That would be all I could ask."

She smiled and brought her hands toward me, touching my mouth with her knuckles experimentally, coyly, to see what I would do. Involuntarily I pulled back, cursing myself as I did so.

If I offended her she didn't show it. "You want something to drink?" she said pleasantly.

"Yes, please."

"Yes, well, what do you want?"

"What? I'm sorry. Scotch and water."

"Okay, Claude." She said my name as if it amused her. "I'll go fix you a drink."

When she came back I had recovered myself but it made me feel foolish to push money toward her. She took it non-committally.

"Do you leave at two?"

"I haven't had any dinner. I'm going to eat here, next door." She pointed through an open door at the other end of the bar. "Will you join me?" she said.

"Only if you'll be my guest."

"That's fine," she said, turning away to serve an anxious customer on my left.

I watched her work for an hour and while I watched I bolted down the four drinks she brought me, one after the other, which, I remarked, kept getting weaker every round.

"We'll have wine with dinner?" she replied.

We had wine with dinner. She ate a forbidding steak, a baked potato, and a salad laden with thick blue-cheese dressing.

I passed the time pushing my fork around in a similar salad, an activity that amused her. "Most men won't eat just a salad," she said.

I explained that I wasn't hungry. She nodded, forking bleeding steak into her mouth and chewing it, with straining jaws, reflectively. "I was starved," she said when she had swallowed. "Tell me about yourself."

"The most interesting thing about me is that I'm having dinner with you."

She nodded, sawing her steak mercilessly. "That's silly," she observed. "Are you married?"

"No. I live alone."

"Have you ever been married?"

"I've not had that good fortune."

"How come?"

"I don't know," I said and it was true, I didn't know. "It never happened."

"That's interesting." She spread a full pat of butter on her potato.

"Have you been married?"

"No. I don't think I'd like it."

"You live alone?"

"As of Monday, I do."

"You had a roommate?"

"I had a leech. I threw him out. I had the locks changed yesterday."

"That sounds like an effective measure." So effective that I considered doing the same myself. Mona, nosy intruder that she was, had a key to my rooms.

Alex took a few swallows of her wine. "The way you talk is funny."

"It pleases you?"

"Why are you so elaborate?"

"I don't know what you mean."

She imitated me, drawing back a bit, then leaning forward as I do. "That sounds like an effective measure."

"What would you have said?"

"I would have said, 'That should work.' "

"Talking to you makes me self-conscious."

"I don't get why you're so hot on me. You don't even know me. I think you've got me figured wrong."

"How do you think I've got you figured?"

"I think you think I'm exciting or exotic or something."

"And you don't think you are."

"You want to see my apartment? That'll give you a good idea of how exciting I am."

"Yes," I said. "I would like to see your apartment."

As you can imagine, I had a dozen motives for my eager acquiescence in this offer and at the bottom of my list was my desire to "see" her apartment. I had already postulated several possible environments for her. She might have youthful middle-class taste—rattan furniture with art-nouveau prints on the walls. She might live among the cast-off furniture of her family, old chairs and couches disguised with Indian bedspreads, fake Oriental rugs, and plants. I hoped there would be no incense but I was prepared for it. I was also steeled for the hard rock with which she would doubtless serenade me. I had a secret hope that she would play Mozart and offer me good sherry in crystal glasses and there would be velvet and leather and even, in some variations, a fire, though it was mid-July and the streets were steaming.

I entertained as many of these fantasies as I could on our walk to her apartment and embellished one by stopping to purchase a bottle of brandy and another of sherry, which I asked her to accept as a token of my regard. At last we arrived at the iron gate and this time the hinges swung squeakily for me and me alone and I passed through. We crossed a dark flagstone courtyard with doors all round and an ex-fountain filled with empty flowerpots at the center, climbed a spidery flight of stairs to a final door, and a second key turned and stripped the darkness from my eyes.

I thought I had covered every possibility. I'd even made a halfhearted nod at early-American eagle-encrusted decor, but I had missed her completely. When she flicked on the light, her arm stretching languidly before me so that for a moment my view was obscured, I saw the place in a flash.

The walls were white, the wooden floor was painted a glossy black, the ceiling was high. It was a large room and the few pieces of furniture only made it appear larger. In one corner a stove, a half-size refrigerator, and a sink competed with one another as if there weren't enough space. On the opposite wall a black and white enamel table sported two white straight-back chairs. The room was L-shaped and at the short end of the L there was a chifforobe and an iron bed, which, I noted at once, was wide enough for two, had two pillows, and was neatly made up with white sheets and a black blanket. Halfway down the long arm of the L was a door, which, I learned later, led to the bathroom, where the floor was white tile and the ceiling was black, an interesting reversal of the pervading color scheme. That was it. No books, no pictures, no plants, no stereo, no TV, no dishes out, no clothes over the chairs, everything as spotless and orderly as a nun's cell. Alex walked in before me and took one of the chairs at the table. "Exotic?" she inquired of the furniture. "Elegant?" of the walls. I stood in the doorway, looking in, and I felt I was looking into a photograph. Alex had propped one foot on the table and busied herself unlacing her boot. Her fingers moved over the laces soundlessly. I noticed the quiet, full and heavy, and I was reluctant to break it by moving or speaking. The place was not what I expected and yet, as I watched her pull off one boot and prop up the other, I could see that she fit into it perfectly, that it was spare, cool, unemotional, and clear. All the qualities that I thought I saw in her were reflected in the room she chose for herself. The place bore me out. I closed the door and went in, clutching my brown paper bag and wondering if there would be any glasses and where I would throw the bag when I took the bottles from it. I sat in the other chair, the only other chair, and put my provisions on the table.

"You don't have to tiptoe, you know," she said.

"Was I?"

"You don't need to whisper, either." She pulled the paper bag from the bottles, picked up her boots, and went to the chifforobe, into which she tossed her boots, carried the bag to the "kitchen," and threw it in a trash can under the sink. From a cabinet over the sink, which I had failed to notice because it was as white as the wall from which it hung, she took two glasses. The cabinet was high and she had to lean over the sink and reach up, her head flung back between her shoulders, her feet stretching up so that I could see the white arches, a position that made her appear vulnerable and transient. I was disoriented. It was so quiet in this room where everything was black or white (my blue socks stood out in my imagination, though I couldn't see them under the table), and I knew myself alone with this lovely young woman who made me feel so old and so childishly giddy all at once. Alex padded back to the table and took her seat across from me.

"I feel very strange," I said.

"I can see that," she replied. She set the brandy bottle between her knees and began to work it open, talking as she occupied herself with the task. "I don't entertain much," she said. "The man who was staying here, he was just here a few days and I couldn't stand it. I couldn't stand his shoes around all the time and the junk he was always putting in the refrigerator. That's silly, I guess, and I think it hurt him when I told him so. He said I was 'resisting our relationship!'" The cork came free and she put the opened bottle on the table. "'Resisting our relationship!'" she snorted. "Can you imagine anyone having the nerve to say something like that."

"Not to you," I said.

She turned the cork over in her fingers, then put it on the table. "Has anyone ever said anything like that to you?"

"Not in those words," I said. I thought of Mona on those futile and painful occasions when we discussed what she called "our future."

Alex poured brandy into the glasses and pushed one toward me. "So for two days I've been alone and now you're here."

"And two days wasn't long enough?" I guessed.

She sipped her drink, looking at me over the glass. "I can never decide," she said calmly, "if it's worse to be alone or with a stranger. Those seem to be the options life is determined to offer me. I don't understand why."

Her melancholy touched and invaded me. I didn't doubt that she chose, in some innocent and oblique way, the loneliness she complained of. Already I could see that she was willing to let me stay or go, whatever I wanted, as long as I didn't leave my things about and try to make her change her solitary ways. I watched her drink the brandy and I knew she was considering what she had said, revising it into something more palatable than the tough course she had outlined. The single bulb that hung from a cord over her head lit her features so that nothing was softened and I could see the fine lines about her eyes, the feathery pale hairs over her lips, the habitual crease in her forehead. I was aware of a prickling sensation in my hands and feet as my circulation ebbed. She set her glass carefully on the table, dug into her pants pocket, and produced two long silver hairpins. She leaned forward a little and caught her hair up at her neck, twisting it into a long black coil and fastening it skillfully with the silver pins, a procedure that was accomplished with grace and speed, changing her whole appearance. Without the voluptuousness of her dark hair, her face was more girlish, delicate, and fragile. She smiled at me. "I was hot," she said.

"Could I ask you to do that again?"

"Do what?"

"With your hair?"

She was wide-eyed. "Take it down and put it back up again?"

"Please."

She pulled the pins out and shook the coil loose about her shoulders. "You've got a lot of ideas," she remarked, pulling her hair through her fingers and winding it back up again.

I had, in fact, so many "ideas" I was afraid my eyes would come popping out of their sockets to relieve the pressure. I applied myself to my brandy in order to hide my growing bemusement.

And then, as if she had hit on a great joke, she offered me torture. "Let's not talk," she suggested, "but let's drink three glasses of this brandy and look at each other and not look away even for a second until we're through."

"No talking?" I asked.

"Not a word. But you can laugh if you have to."

"I'm ready," I said.

We drank and looked. I dare not guess what she saw in my

face but it made her smile. I feasted upon her features, study-ing the almond curve of her eyes, the blue-veined lids and dark lashes, the flecks of silver in the pale green iris, the shiny black of her pupils. I spent some time over the bridge of her nose and in examining the curve of her dark brows. Her upper lip delighted me, the cleft long and shallow, flaring slightly at her mouth. Her lips were parted, and as I watched the moist ivory line of her teeth, they parted too and the end of her tongue appeared, wet and inviting, to tease the edge of the glass she brought to her mouth. "I'm going to laugh," she said.

"No talking."

"How can you look so hard and not laugh?"

"No laughing, no talking," I said.

"I'm ready for another glass."

I filled her glass. She sipped it dutifully. "It's going to my head," she said. "I'm giddy. I don't think I should drink another."

"It was your plan," I reminded her. "You have to stick it out."

"Come on," she protested. "You haven't even finished that one glass."

I poured the burning contents of my glass down my throat.

"You're going to be sorry you did that."

"No, no," I insisted while the flames whipped up to my brain and my vision clouded. "Stick to your bargain, miss, and keep still."

She squirmed in her seat. "I can't. This chair is too un-comfortable. Let's sit somewhere else."

Again she accomplished with straightforward ease the move I hadn't the courage to make, for there was one other place to sit in her simple apartment and that, as we both knew, was the bed. She stood up and led me to it.

It was a long way across that room and in my journey I had all the fears any man has ever had. Out there in what looked and felt like a void was a bed, and between it and me a strange and beautiful woman turned and beckoned me. And I had offered her my services. My vanity confounded me. I might as well offer a star assistance in lighting the heavens. The brandy kept my blood from turning to ice but I dreaded what my intoxicated state might or might not produce when I reached my destination. Alex sat on the edge of the bed, her feet flat on the floor, and turned to me, smoothing the sheet beside her with her palm, giving me a hopeful friendly smile that turned into a laugh when she saw my face. "You sure look like a troubled man," she said.

I sat at her side, holding my glass with both hands. "Deeply troubled," I confessed.

She rested her head on my arm, weak from the brandy and probably not expecting much from me. "Me, too," she said. "I'm deeply troubled."

The events that followed this doleful exchange made me forget not only my troubles but most of my life. Alex's unexpected delicacy inspired me with tenderness and my fears vanished. She was delighted with my performance and I admit to being pleased with myself. Such powerful and satisfying passion had not so emboldened or sustained me in a long time and I felt like shouting out or dancing across her shiny black floor. "Claude," she said, grazing her warm lips back and forth against my chest, "you are such a nice surprise." I was happy and safe and didn't want to leave, but I thought I'd better not push my luck. I certainly couldn't have slept. Alex grew quiet at my side. Then she began to fidget about, getting comfortable. "I'm sleepy," she said. "I can't stay awake. Thank you for a lovely evening."

I laughed. "Are we at the door?"

"Huh?"

"Go to sleep," I said. "I'll be gone when you wake up."

"You can stay if you want."

"And risk your wrath at the sight of my shoes on the floor? No thanks."

"You're a good listener," she observed, turning away from

me. I lay still for a while, watching her slow breathing. Then I got up, dressed, and slipped out quietly.

Outside, the air was hot and clear, the stars were pinpoints of ice, and the moon was halfway up the sky. My feet were light and my mind raced so fast I had to put my hands over my eyes to try to calm myself. "I hope I don't have a heart attack," I said to my palms. I decided to walk home, fifty unforgettable blocks.

What I discovered about myself that night was the beginning of the change in me. (For I am a changed man.) I discovered that I possess a great capacity for happiness. Of course I had suspected it. I've always been subject to fits of elation that come without cause or purpose and leave me gasping for air. Not long ago I was walking on St. Charles when two young women passed me, both wearing bathing suits with sweat shirts pulled on top, and as I considered their long tan bare legs and noted that they were wearing identical sandals, the smell of chlorine assailed me and my heart was flooded with joy. This was the same pleasure, but it lasted and lasted. When I felt it wavering, I had only to recall Alex's blouse slipping from her shoulders, or the way she had turned her head shyly so that her hair, coming loose from the pins, fell across her breasts, or the warmth in her eyes when, after the last bit of cloth was gone between us and I, taking courage to really look at my unwrapped gift, said, "Well" (for she was lovely beyond description), she laughed, reaching out to me. "Don't stare," she said, pulling me down.

I reached my door too soon. My legs were tired and I wanted to lie down but I hated to leave the clear sky and warm scented air. I stood on my doorstep for a few moments. Then I went inside and went to bed.

The next evening I returned to the bar but Alex wasn't there. The young man who replaced her told me it was her night off. I left my name and my phone number and went away feeling chastised. Suppose she didn't call? I thought of going to her apartment but if she wasn't alone I wouldn't have known what to do with myself. I passed the next day in alternating fits of anxiety and optimism. That night, I pretended to read a book while I sat next to my phone, turning the pages mindlessly until, at one-fifteen, it rang.

"Claude, it's me, Alex," she said.

"What a relief," I replied, clutching the receiver to my ear.

"Sorry about last night," she said. "I didn't know how to reach you."

"I know. That's why I left the note."

"What are you doing? Are you coming down tonight?"

"If you want me to," I said, "I'm on my way."

"Good." She laughed. "Honey, what's your last name."

"It's Ledet," I said. "What's yours?"

"Tate," she said. "See you soon." She hung up.

I pulled on my shirt and ran out to the street, where a streetcar stood waiting on the neutral ground and the moon bathed the scene in dreamy light, cool and mysterious.

3

She was waiting at the door when I arrived. "Let's go," she said. "I'm sick of this place."

I walked along beside her. "Why do you work there?" I inquired.

"It's easy. The money's okay. I'm used to it." She paused, giving me a suspicious sidelong look. "Does it bother you?"

"No," I said. "It suits you. I can't imagine you doing anything else."

"You're strange," she said, slipping her arm about my waist, apparently pleased with my answer. I drew her closer, holding her against me and breathing in the dusky fragrance of her hair. "When I woke up and you were gone, it was so strange," she said.

"What did you think?"

"It's like a dream I'm having. I thought, did I dream it? And then I saw the glasses on the table."

We walked on without talking. I felt myself relaxing. Waiting for her call, hurrying to her, I had been in a turmoil, but now I was calm and as cool as her silky neck, which I nuzzled through her hair. A sense of elation filled me, buoying me up, and I thought if I could only walk along forever with my face in her hair and her strong body fitted against my own, I would be content. There was nothing strident, nothing hysterical, none of that keenness that I had always felt with women, that gleaming edge that makes me think I must do something, say something, be something. I had no desire to explain myself. We walked along quietly until we arrived at her gate. She gave me the key, still leaning against me. We crossed the courtyard and climbed the staircase, our arms still intertwined. At the door she paused and turned to me, raising her face to be kissed, her eyes already half closed, her lips slightly parted, and I embraced her. She was slow to release me, slow to lead me inside. She didn't bother to turn on the light but, taking my hand, led me through the darkness to her bed. We sat, side by side, and she sighed, leaning against me. Then she reached down and pulled at the laces of her boots.

"Let me do that," I said. I sat on the floor and took her feet into my lap. I took my time over the laces, loosening each one carefully, then slipping each boot off and laying them to one side. She sat very still. Her feet were bare and I fitted my hand across the arch, pressing the long tendon with a circular motion. Her long toes curled down, then flexed out and apart. "That feels wonderful," she said. "My feet ache." I caressed her ankles, circling the hard bone with my tongue and trying my teeth on the Achilles tendon. She drew her fingers through my hair, rubbing my skull with the same motion I applied to her arches. "I'm curious about you," she said.

"What do you want to know?"

She fell back on the bed and addressed the ceiling. "Oh, I don't know. What are you like? What do you do? Do you have a bad temper? Are you obstinate?"

I stood up and leaned over her, spreading her hair out on the pillow. I arranged it so that it all came to one side and a few strands reached her shoulders. I took her chin between my thumb and forefinger and adjusted her head, first to one side, then the other. She watched me curiously.

"I work for the government," I whispered, bringing my face close to hers. "And I have the patience of Job."

She laughed, wrapping her arms and legs around me in one quick motion so that I collapsed across her.

After she was asleep I sat up and rubbed my eyes with the heels of my hands. I was weary and wanted to lie back and sleep beside her. I dragged myself to my feet and dressed in the dark, carrying my shoes outside, where I sat on the stair landing and tugged them onto my feet. My feelings were in an uproar. My strongest desire, which startled me, was to go back to her, to wake her up and make her open the door I had so foolishly closed behind me. I knew this course was impossible, that its result would be disastrous, and that certainty made me sit still. I tried to examine my uneasiness. This night was different from the first night. Our lovemaking then had surprised me, purely because of the improbability of it happening at all. I had stumbled into more than I had hoped for and I was delighted. But I hadn't expected the repetition of the act to be more confounding, more stimulating, more satisfying. If things continued at this pace I would surely expire in Alex's arms in the next week or so, a happy dead man. She had been less shy, more playful, but still there was a delicacy, a reticence, something tentatively withheld that I felt I must have, must go back and find. The progress of my life had always been this, having less and craving less. I felt I was undergoing a kind of reverse aging, and though I enjoyed it, I had the good sense to fear it. I had more, I wanted more.

I wandered down across the courtyard and out into the street. It was four in the morning by the time I got home and I fell into bed, too exhausted to take off my clothes. I was drifting into sleep when the phone rang.

"Claude," Mona said breathlessly. "Thank God you're home. I was worried to death."

I glanced at the clock behind me. It was four-twenty.

"Why are you calling me at this hour?" I inquired sensibly.

"I've been calling for hours. Where have you been?"

"I was out walking. I couldn't sleep."

"I had this horrible dream about you. You were lying in the street and some Negroes had cut off your hands. I woke up in a panic, it was so real. So *real*, Claude. Are you sure you're all right?"

I looked at my hands. "You're calling me to tell me your dream?"

"I woke up afraid. I knew it was silly but I thought I'd call just to make sure you were all right, and then when you didn't answer for hours I didn't know what to think."

"I see," I said. "Well, I'm fine. I appreciate your calling."

"I'm sorry," she said. "It's so late. But while I've got you, I was thinking of dinner Saturday night. The cook from Le Boucher has moved to the Mouton and they say it's such a lovely room."

I tried to think fast but failed. I realized I was about to say no but I couldn't see any further into the future than that.

"I can't," I said. "I'm busy Saturday."

There was a meaningful pause in our conversation.

"Everything is becoming so difficult between us, don't you feel that?" she said.

"It is difficult," I agreed.

"I've been giving it a lot of thought and I've decided it's because we live too far apart and you don't have a car."

My mind was wandering. I knew she was leading me somewhere I didn't want to go, but I didn't care. "I can't afford a car," I said.

"I know. I know you can't. That's why I've decided to move into the city. Somewhere in walking distance from you."

My throat contracted and something in my stomach turned over. "Can't we talk about this later?" I said. "I can call you tomorrow."

"There's nothing to talk about. My mind's made up. In

fact, I have two appointments to look at apartments tomorrow. I'll just sell the house. After all, it's mine to sell."

I knew that if I wasn't so tired I would have been angry. Instead, I began to feel sad. Mona dreaded life in the city. It was fun to come in in the evenings, but the suburbs were safer, cleaner, and there were no Negroes. She had decided to give up everything she knew and risk her safety and her fortune on me. I thought of Alex and I was sadder still.

"I'm very tired, Mona," I said. "I want to talk to you about this but I want to do it when I'm alert."

"Nothing's wrong, is it, dear? You are pleased?"

Maybe three or four times in my life a woman has pulled me up on a hook like this. I always manage to ease my way free with a combination of guile and slipperyness, but every time it happens I fear that I will fail. That fear drove me on and I determined to settle with Mona at once. "Something *is* wrong," I said, "and I am not pleased."

"Oh," she said. "I . . ." She tried to make a joke of it. "I can move where I please, I guess."

"Mona," I said. "I won't ever marry you. I won't even live in the same house with you and I resent your trying to force me to do so."

"I'm not trying to force you to do anything," she exclaimed. "You're forcing me."

I knew better than to pursue such a line of reasoning but I was curious to see just how she would maintain it. "How am I forcing you?" I inquired.

"You're forcing me to give up my house and all my possessions and everything I love, to please your selfishness. You don't care how much I worry about you. I was mad with worry and you don't even care enough to tell me where you were. I certainly don't believe you were walking around on the street for four hours. I fail to see why you can't think of me a little, Claude. I don't ask for much. I give you everything I have and I don't begrudge it to you, I give it willingly. But you only think of yourself, nothing but yourself."

I decided she deserved the truth. "I'm thinking of another woman," I said. "And I was with another woman."

"Oh my God," she whispered. "After all I've done for you."

"I did appreciate all the dinners," I said.

"I never want to speak to you again," she exclaimed. There was an awkward silence, which I refused to disturb, in order to help her keep the vow she had just made. Then she hung up.

I knew she wasn't done with me but I was pleased with myself for having initiated our separation. She was good enough to let me sleep for the few hours I had left before I had to be at work. I expected an 8 a.m. call at the office but she surprised me by showing up in person at lunchtime. She waved to me through the glass partition that separates the accountants from the secretaries, cheerful and smiling, though when she was closer I saw that her upper lip was wet with perspiration.

"Can we have lunch?" she asked nervously. "I just had to come. I felt so bad about our conversation last night."

I put a paperweight on my latest projection for the future cost of Social Security and followed her out into the hall without comment.

"Let's go to the Papillon," she suggested.

"I thought you hated the Papillon."

"I don't hate it. The kitchen isn't what it might be but it's a lovely room and the service is good."

"I can't afford it," I said.

"It doesn't matter. I have my American Express card."

We went to the Papillon, where I ate a fish wrapped around a mushroom and Mona picked at a dish of creamed crabmeat while she apologized for being so rude the night before.

"I didn't think you were rude," I said when she was out of breath.

"What?" She tried to second-guess me, failed. "I said terrible things and I wanted you to know I didn't mean them."

"I see," I said. "But I *meant* the things I said."

She rubbed the back of her hand against her forehead and her eyes closed briefly, trying to shut out what she now saw was inevitable. "I don't remember what you said," she confessed.

My throat ached with a lump of pity for her but a bite of my mushroom pushed it away. "Mona, dear," I said, taking her hands over the table, "I know this is hard on you. I wish I could make it easier, but I can't."

"Is it something I've done?"

"Nothing. Nothing to do with you."

"It's this other woman."

"I'm afraid so."

"Is she young?"

"She's thirty."

She drew her hands away from me and covered her face with them. "Oh God," she said softly.

I knew what she was thinking. It was in all the women's magazines. Men my age were like overripe plums, falling into the laps of young women all over the country. My ego was involved in some damnable way. This young woman would make me feel important in ways that Mona could not imitate. And what was worse, the young woman wouldn't see my worth, would walk all over me and cast me off when she was tired of me, and then I would come crawling back, sadder, wiser, older. The vision I had of Mona's thoughts gave me a chill and I chewed my fish listlessly, a condemned man.

Before she could respond, the waitress approached the table. "Do you want dessert?" she asked.

Mona nodded sleepily. "Custard," she said. "And coffee."

"And you, sir?"

I pushed my plate away impatiently. "Coffee," I said.

Mona waited until the waitress was out of earshot. "I suppose you think I'll just wait for you."

"I certainly don't expect that."

She laughed. "Don't you? Don't you? You think I don't know what you're doing."

"I don't see how you could. I'm not certain myself."

"Oh, how sad. How very sad." She warmed to her part. "I wish someone would hurt you the way you've hurt me."

"It's useless for us to pursue this line of thought," I suggested.

The waitress arrived with our coffee. Mona gave her cup a look of hostility and distaste. She took a bag of sugar from the saucer and tore it vengefully, but her hands were shaking. The sugar spilled into her lap. "This is too much," she shouted, rising from her seat and shoving the chair back behind her with a vicious kick. "It's too much to be borne." She turned from the table, whirled across the room, and was out the door before I could remind her that she hadn't paid the check.

The waitress hurried over and picked up Mona's chair. "Is everything all right?" she asked sympathetically.

"I'm afraid not," I said. "She's taken the credit card with her and I don't have enough money on me to pay this check."

"Oh dear," she said. "What will you do?"

"I thought I might have another cup of coffee," I said.

She looked around her, as if asking permission of the air, then brought the coffeepot to my table and filled my cup. "Perhaps you could leave something as security," she suggested. "A watch or something."

I showed her my bare and freckled wrists. "Don't worry," I said. "I'll come up with something."

She went away, leaving me to solve my problem at my leisure. I drank my coffee, looked about the restaurant, feeling inexplicably gay. Mona, I thought, would probably take one more stab at me but I felt confident of my ability to fend her off. I noticed she had left her custard untouched and I helped myself to it greedily. My gentle waitress watched me worriedly from a post across the room. It touched me to see her agitation. As she exchanged a few words with a fellow waitress, I realized she hadn't told anyone of my predicament. I raised my finger and she was at my side in a moment.

"Here's my plan," I said. "I'm going to call a friend at my office a few blocks away and he'll bring me some money to pay for this delicious meal."

She nodded compliantly.

I pointed to a series of canopies in the lobby. "Right over there," I said, "are a number of phones. You will watch me make my call and then I'll come back and have another cup of this excellent coffee until my friend arrives."

"That will be fine, sir," she said, thus securing for herself the largest tip I have ever left.

I went to the phone and called David, feeling justified in doing so as it was he who had introduced me to Mona and so put me on the path to my present misfortune. He agreed to bail me out in return for the details of my difficulties with Mona. I returned to the table and gave my waitress a nod. I decided that I would go immediately home after work and sleep until it was time to get up and go to Alex.

In a few minutes David arrived, clucking and petulant as a mother hen. He paid my check and I thanked my waitress for her patience. Outside, he couldn't wait to begin his friendly prying.

"She just walked out on you? What did you say to upset her?"

"I told her I was seeing another woman and that I wished to discontinue our eating arrangements."

"Christ," he exclaimed. "Why did you do that? What a shit you are sometimes. It's no wonder you have to live alone."

"I did that because it's true. And I'm not all alone and even if I were it wouldn't bother me. Mona drives me crazy, as you know."

"She's lonely and she loves you. Why don't you marry her?"

"I don't like her."

We stood on Poydras Street watching the traffic speed by. When the light changed, David bolted into the street as if he wanted to get away from me. I maintained my turtle pace and he waited for me at the curb.

"You're my oldest friend," he advised me. "But I don't understand what you're doing. Do you really have another woman lined up?"

I thought of Alex and I was annoyed at the tone my day was taking. She was not "another woman." She was my extraordinary secret woman and I had committed more to her in a few days than I had to anyone in my life. I didn't believe it was my age, my inveterate isolation, my failing ego. I thought it was my extreme good fortune and nothing more.

"David," I said to my old friend and sometime confidant, "mind your own business."

He slapped his forehead with his hand. "I believe you've cracked, old boy. Who is this woman? I want to meet her."

"Never," I said. "Never in your life."

He changed his tack. "What can I tell Candy? Mona's her best friend, her dearest friend. Suppose she comes over tonight to cry on our shoulders. What will I say?"

"Say whatever you want," I whined. "Do what you want. I don't care about Mona. I'm a free man and I don't care."

It was hot on the street and I felt I was suffocating, had been suffocating for years. The idea of returning to my desk and putting off David's nervous inquiries for the rest of the afternoon made me want to turn and run. My brain, like a printing press gone mad, churned out pictures of Alex. I saw her bending over me, arching her back beneath me, turning away from me. Then I was treated to close-ups: her long feet, her shoulder blades sharp beneath the taut flesh, her smooth breasts, her fleshy earlobes, her white thighs tensed so that the muscle raised against my probing fingers, her wide knowledgeable eyes—one after the other visions flooded over me and I felt sweat breaking out on my forehead. I was a free man all right and I wanted to do one thing with my freedom: lay it at Alex's feet and invite her to tread upon it, useless and fragile stuff that it was.

I pulled at my tie frantically. David turned sympathetic. "You're upset," he said. "It's embarrassing to be stuck in a restaurant with no money."

I laughed.

"Did Mona know you didn't have any money?"

"That bitch," I said.

"She was good enough for you when you had no one else," he pointed out. "Her money was good enough for you, too."

"She told me repeatedly that she gave herself and her cash freely, without hope of repayment."

David lapsed into chastened silence. When we arrived at the office I thanked him for coming to my rescue.

"Sure," he said. "No trouble. If you need me for anything, just call." He went to his desk and didn't speak to me for the rest of the day.

I spent my afternoon building up a good rage. I thought of all the things I should have said to Mona and fumed over the possibility of David intruding himself into my relations with Alex. When I left the office the sky was overcast and this suited me. I went to my apartment, threw the windows open, and crawled gratefully into my bed. When I woke up, six hours later, it was raining heavily, great sheets of water illumined by soundless flashes of heat lightning. I bathed, shaved, and dressed, fried a pork chop, which I ate with my fingers, and after digging through the closet for my favorite possession, a push-button umbrella as black as my mood, I went out into the storm to find Alex.

The bar was crowded with damp impatient patrons, the floor was slick and dirty. Alex was turning out drinks as fast as she could and barely had time to say hello. Her shift was to end at two, but Pete, her replacement (she told me quickly as she shoved a drink my way), had called to say he would be late. She had to restock the beer coolers herself, hauling ten heavy cases behind the bar. I offered to help her but she cut me off and told me to wait on the other side of the bar. As she was opening the last case she cut her hand on the metal cording. She winced and cursed, then pressed her bleeding palm to her lips, sucking off the sudden blood. She finished unloading the case, oblivious to the orders directed at her from the bar.

She was running water over her hand when the man came in. He was drunk and pushed his way up to the bar, insulting anyone who crossed his path. Alex ignored him and he stood at the bar, drumming a coin on the counter, wet, impatient, and vicious. Alex passed in front of him on her way to the first-aid kit and again on her way back. She took an order from a woman a few seats down, then made her third pass in front of the infuriated man. Suddenly he reached across the bar and grabbed her arm so that she was forced to turn to him. "What's the matter, honey," he said. "You don't see me here?" Alex went pale and her mouth tightened grimly. I left my seat and started moving toward the man, though he was so much bigger than I, I don't know what I thought I was going to do. I had to walk away from the bar to get through the crowd, and as I did I saw, to my relief, that Pete was coming in the door.

After that, everything happened quickly. Alex hissed something at the man, I didn't hear what it was. She tried to free herself from his grip but he hung on, leaning far over the bar so that one foot left the floor. She looked toward the door, I think she saw Pete, and then she looked behind her. I was close to them both by this time. The crowd, sensing violence, parted and I had a clear view of Alex. With her free arm she reached toward the shelf where the glasses were kept. She could have chosen any one, there were all kinds. Her hand paused, moved over the glasses to the left, then quickly to the right. It settled on a beer stein, thick glass with a heavy solid base. She turned on the man. He had his head down over her arm, his mouth pressed against the crook of her elbow. She lifted the glass high over her head.

I saw her face clearly and what I saw surprised me. There was no fear, no panic. Her eyes were flat and cold and her lips were pulled back from her teeth in a smile. The room was hushed and for a split second all eyes turned in her direction and all breathing stopped. Over the confused and motionless crowd her face floated, like the moon over the silent whirling earth, beautiful, still, serene, and relentless. She brought the glass down, with all her strength, across the base of his skull.

The man slumped across the bar, then fell back into Pete's arms. Pete dragged him behind the bar and threw water in his face. Alex stood behind him, watching indifferently. I approached the bar and looked down at the unconscious man. He lay quiet on the dirty floor, his mouth open, his eyes closed peacefully. Alex stepped over him and came out into the crowd looking for me. "Let's get out of here," she said when she reached me.

"Shouldn't we stay and see if he comes out of it?" I asked.

"Pete can handle it," she said and walked quickly toward the door. I looked over the bar again and saw the man sputter, groan, and turn over on his side. Pete pulled him roughly to a sitting position, then turned to me. "He's all right," he said. I backed away, dazed by what I had seen, and followed Alex out into the street.

I stumbled along at her side for a block without speaking. She walked purposefully and didn't seem to know I was with her. "He's all right," I said. "He was coming to. I saw him."

"That stupid son-of-a-bitch," she said, without emotion. "If Pete hadn't come in when he did I would have killed him."

"Jesus, Alex," I said. "What came over you?"

"I don't know," she said. Then, coldly, "Did I shock you?"

I had been surprised by her unequivocal decisiveness, by the way she had paused over those glasses and chosen, automatically, the one that would do the most damage, and by the way she had determined without question that she

43

would eliminate entirely the obstacle that annoyed her. That surprised me, perhaps it shocked me, but I admired her for it. I thought she had done the right thing and done it well. If the man had died on the floor before my eyes I would have felt the same way. "No," I said sincerely. "I thought you did the right thing."

She turned to me, smiled at me. "You really mean that, don't you."

"Yes."

She stopped, looked up and down the street, then, wrapping her arms about my waist, pulled me into the shadows. "Come here," she said, smiling mischievously. "I'll shock you."

That night, instead of turning away, she fell asleep in my arms. I held her loosely, adjusting my breathing to hers, slow and effortless. We lay on top of the sheets, my back propped up with pillows against the wall. Her hair was spread out artfully across my chest, her arms flung wide, as if she had fallen upon me from a great height. Her long body stretched out away from mine but I could barely make it out, it was so dark in her windowless rooms. I felt a sense of dread, starting deep in my brain and vibrating out to fill my head, my body, all my senses. I didn't want to leave. I wanted to stay. If some phantom had risen up and offered me an infernal contract in exchange for stopping time dead for a few years, I would have signed eagerly.

I dreaded time and knew it for our enemy. I could hear it in the air I breathed, moving in and out of my lungs, nagging and complaining, like a bad wife. I wanted no part of it. Alex parted her dry lips in her sleep, then pressed them together again, innocent and far away from me. She lifted me out of time. I floated away, reluctant at first, worried, afraid to make a mistake, any little mistake that might cost me my present happiness. I fought a little but not as hard as I should have. When I woke up I found my clothes folded neatly on the bed beside me and Alex nowhere in sight.

4

I sat up and looked around. I could smell coffee and there was a humming sound in the air. After a moment I realized that it was running water and that it was coming from the bathroom. I dressed hurriedly and looked for a clock, which I found built into the stove. I had fifteen minutes to get to work. Should I tell her I was leaving or would it be better to have her come out and find me gone? I stood halfway between the kitchen and bedroom, longing for a cup of coffee and toying with the dark possibility that it was Saturday. Was it Saturday? I couldn't remember. The bathroom door opened and Alex stepped out, wrapped in a towel and preceded by a rush of steamy warm air, her bare feet leaving damp tracks on the shiny black floor.

"You're up," she observed.

"Is it Saturday?"

"Sure," she said. She went to the kitchen, poured herself a cup of coffee, and sipped it ruefully. "I'm going back to bed," she said. "Want to come?"

I felt her displeasure. "No thanks," I said. "I'm leaving. Call me when you want me."

"I need some sleep," she replied, pouring the remains of her coffee down the drain. She leaned against the counter, warm and flushed from her bath, but impatient, petulant. "I'll want you tomorrow," she said. "If that's convenient." She examined the fingernails of one hand, then looked at me archly. I thought she was like a girl who has sensed for the first time the extent of her power and is compelled to test it, not because she is vicious, but as an experiment. I smiled.

"What's funny?" she asked, annoyed by my smile.

"I feel," I said, "that I'm about to play the moth to your flame."

"And that makes you smile?"

"I was thinking that the moth is never thought to be courageous. It's assumed that he's a fool."

"I always think he has no choice."

"Yes," I said. "That's true."

She shifted her weight from one foot to the other. "How old are you anyway, Claude?"

"Forty-nine," I said.

Her eyes widened and she pushed out her lower lip speculatively. "No shit," she said. I saw to my relief that though she was surprised she wasn't dismayed. In fact, the idea seemed to amuse her. I stood quietly, waiting to be dismissed, hoping to be called back.

"Come sit at the table," she said. "I have something I need to discuss with you."

"Only if you give me some of that coffee," I said.

She fluttered like a negligent hostess. "I'm sorry," she said. "I'm so rude." She followed me to the table and set a cup before me.

"I want sugar in it," I said.

She grimaced. "You would." She went to the counter and returned with a small jar of sugar and a teaspoon. "Everything all right now?" she said. "All set?"

"I don't know. Is this going to be bad news?"

"That depends on you." She opened a drawer beneath the tabletop and took out an envelope. "Read this," she said. "It's self-explanatory."

The envelope was addressed to her in a meticulous feminine hand, each letter appearing to have been formed with equal attention. I removed the folded sheet of paper gingerly.

"Go ahead," Alex said. "Read it."

I read: "Dear Alexis."

"Is your name Alexis?" I asked.

"No. It's Alexandra. That's her name for me."

I returned my attention to the letter.

Dear Alexis,

I am now huge with the illegitimate heir to the family fortune and my presence has become a liability at social functions as well as breakfast. The parents entreat me to remove my unsightliness to Beaufort and I have agreed to do so on the condition that I may have you and Collie with me. Collie is an easy matter but you will be, as usual, more difficult. Mother says, please, she hopes you are well and she would consider it an honor to undertake any expenses you might incur in return for the great service you will render the family by joining me in my confinement. And I say, not please, but you must. I refuse to go through this without you. I am engaging a doctor who will teach you how to deliver my baby. Collie will be your assistant and the three of us will muddle through as best we can, as we have done so often in the past.

I want you for four months at least. Collie and I leave tomorrow. I'm taking the boat. Send a wire to the house naming the time and date and I will fly across the water and steal you away.

Oh yes, if you have an unassuming and unsuspecting man you'd care to bring along, please do so. I respect your appetites as you know, and besides we will have none of that sex there except the inebriated Banjo, who won't come near the house such is his fear of the combined forces of Collie and me. Suppose the plumbing breaks or we have to re-wire something.

A man or a manual, whichever comes easiest. Only say you will come quickly to your affectionate and needy

Diana

I finished the letter, then read it again. "Who is she?" I

asked, folding the paper and replacing it in its creamy vellum envelope.

"A friend of mine," she said. "My oldest friend. She's rich."

"And you're going to stay with her."

"Yes," she said. "I'm leaving Friday."

"What about your job?"

"I'll quit it. They'll take me back when I get back."

"And the apartment?"

"I lock the door."

"And you'll be gone four months."

"It'll probably be six, if I know Diana. And I do."

I placed the letter before me on the table, succumbing to a feeling of helplessness. Six months was not a long time but I felt the days stretching out before me endless and empty. And Alex, I thought, was only relieved to have found such an easy way of being rid of me. "I see," I said.

"My feet are cold," she said. "Would you give me your socks?"

I pulled off my shoes wearily and handed her the socks across the table, noting with pleasure as I did so that they were a matched pair and had no holes. Alex pulled them over her feet. "So," she said. "Will you come with me?"

I considered my own bare feet. The horny nails needed clipping. "I can't," I said, annoyed with her for making me say it. "I have a job."

"Can't you quit it."

"No. I couldn't go back and I would have difficulty finding another at my age."

"Wouldn't you get some retirement or something?"

"Alex," I said, taking her hand, "I can't just go running off to someplace I never heard of. You'd be tired of me in a week and then where would I be?"

"Take the chance," she said. "Do you think you'll get another one like this?"

I sat in stubborn silence.

"I've got to get dressed," she said. "I'm cold."

She stood up and came to my chair, wrapping her arms around my shoulders and pressing her face against my neck. She spoke softly, close to my ear. "I want you to come with me. I don't want to go by myself and I want you with me."

I thought of going to the office on Monday morning and filling out a resignation slip. That would be all there was to it. I would receive, after twenty-five years of faithful dogged service, a small pension, scarcely enough to live on. But there was my savings account, which I had been hoarding for all those years, living frugally and watching the balance climb, telling no one. I had 80,000 dollars in that account. Enough to live on for years.

Alex released me and went to the chifforobe. She took out jeans, a black T-shirt, and a pair of lacy blue pants, returned to the table, and put the clothes down in front of me. Then she unfastened her towel and threw it toward me with a flourish. It landed on my head and I didn't bother to remove it. It was damp and fragrant and I closed my eyes, inhaling deeply.

"Are you sulking?" she asked.

"No," I said. "I'm trying to make up my mind."

"Good. Does the towel help?"

"Yes, it smells like you." It wasn't bad under the towel. My life, I thought, was becoming a series of moments I didn't want to end. I could hear Alex dressing, and because I didn't wish to miss the moment when she would zip her jeans and stretch her arms up to put on her shirt, I pulled the towel from my face.

"Have you made up your mind?" she asked.

"What does she mean by 'unsuspecting'?"

She zipped and snapped the jeans, then raised her arms, pulling the shirt down over her head, her back arched and turned slightly toward me. It was a fine sight. "Unsuspecting?" she said.

49

"In the letter. She says you can bring an unsuspecting man."

"Where?" She picked up the letter and scanned it.

"Penultimate paragraph," I said.

She scowled at me. Her eyes moved over the page slowly. Too slowly, I thought. She couldn't find the word. She held the letter out to me. "Where?"

I pointed to the sentence. "An unassuming and unsuspecting man," I read.

She shrugged. "That's just the way she talks. She's worse than you. You'll get along fine with her. You'll love her."

I looked at the handwriting and tried to hide my surprise at the discovery I had just made, that Alex knew I had made. Later she was to confess it to me, impatiently, ironically. Though she *could* read when she had to, she did so only with the greatest difficulty.

"What does Diana look like?" I said.

"She's tall, pretty. Athletic."

I pictured such a person. "I think I would only be in the way," I said.

Alex pulled her chair next to mine and sat down. "This is really stupid. I've gone and gotten dressed and I meant to go back to bed."

"I should go," I said. "I'm making you nervous."

"No. Not until you decide." There was about her an urgency, a brooding uneasiness that I couldn't fathom.

"Why me?" I said.

"I know it's soon for us to be doing something like this. But I'm certain it will be all right."

"What makes you certain."

"There's something about you. I don't know. Sometimes I think you're shy, then I think you're very sure of yourself."

"It's possible to be both."

"I don't think you would push me to do anything. I think you would leave me alone."

"I see," I said. But I didn't see. It annoys me when people

think they can depend on me to be what I appear to be, and I think my disgruntlement is sensible. But at the same time my curiosity was seriously aroused. How would it be if I went to this place with her? I didn't wish to cause her trouble, or find myself trapped and troubled, but I did want to find out how it would be. She was right when she suggested that I take the chance because I wouldn't get such another. The thing was possible, it was something I could do and such an opportunity had never come my way before. I did not doubt that it would never come again. I spent a few moments thinking it over while Alex drummed her fingers absentmindedly on my knee. Then I said, "All right. I'll go."

She straddled my lap and kissed me heartily, such was her pleasure at having her own way.

That is how I came to give up my job, my shabby but secure apartment (which I had lived in for fifteen years), my dull friends and duller mistress, everything and everyone I knew. I left all this behind to go to a place I had never seen, with a woman I hardly knew.

When I put it that way I am an adventurer but, of course, I know that I'm not. I made my big step in a series of little steps and the transition to Beaufort was uneventful.

First I quit my job. Monday morning I was at work early. I went to the supply room and found a stack of resignation forms. An X here, a signature there, it was simple. There was another form which requested all my leave pay and another asking me to indicate the way in which I wished to receive my retirement. I brought these forms to my supervisor and told him that I would not return to work after Friday. He expressed first his surprise, then his dismay, but neither of these emotions overwhelmed him and we concluded our interview with expressions of our mutual esteem. He didn't ask me why I was leaving and for this courtesy I was grateful.

An hour later David was at my desk. "What's going on?" he exclaimed. "Have you resigned?"

I pulled a chair up to my desk and offered it to my old

friend. I had decided to tell him the truth, as I didn't see the need for anything less, but I knew he wouldn't be able to take it without sitting down. I offered him a cigarette, which he accepted greedily. "Yes," I said. "I've resigned. I'm leaving town for a while."

"You're leaving? Have you got another job?"

"No. I'm going away with Alex."

He took a long drag from his cigarette and held it in his mouth until I began to worry. Then he expelled it suddenly. "With that girl?" he said.

"She's a grown woman with a mind of her own."

"Are you marrying her?"

"No. Look, David. It's sudden and I have to move fast and I could honestly use your help as soon as you get over the shock."

"Sure," he said obligingly. "Sure. You can count on me. I just can't get over it. You've quit. Just like that. They won't take you back, you know."

"I know."

"Damn," he said, puffing again. "Damn. Who will I talk to around here?"

"I won't miss this place much," I said.

"No." He looked around at the typing secretaries, the gray walls, the rows of files. "Jesus, I envy you. Tell me how this happened."

I told him the little I knew and he furrowed his brow and pressed his lips together as if he could think of nothing more interesting, more important, than my little story.

"I've got to see this woman," he said when I had concluded. "Before you go, huh. Let me just see her."

"I don't see how," I said. "I'm leaving on Friday."

"Jesus. Friday. This Friday?" It was too much for him.

"I've got to clear out my apartment," I said. "You know what it's like."

"I could bring the truck over."

"Yes," I said. "Tonight, if you can. It'll take two nights at least."

"You going to put your stuff in storage?"

I had a clear and perfect vision of how to solve my big problem, which was getting rid of the accumulated crap of my life. I would pile it all into David's big truck and take it to a dump. I felt wonderful, free, reckless. "I'm going to throw it away," I said.

David was practical. "What about your books?"

"You can have those," I said. "And anything else that strikes your fancy."

"This is fantastic," he concluded. "This is insane."

He arrived at seven that evening and we began dismantling my rooms. We worked ourselves into a sweat, hauling out my heavy desk, a metal kitchen cabinet, a bookcase. David had thought to bring boxes for my books and two six-packs of beer. We took a break after packing the books and sat on the front stair drinking beer. David was continually giving me shy, sidelong glances, like a woman trying to comprehend the whim of her mate, anxious and eager to hit just the right note.

"What about Mona?" he said.

"I haven't seen her. I've stopped answering the phone."

He nodded. "I wish I hadn't seen her."

"She's bothering you?"

"She's been over every fifteen minutes since that lunch thing. She cries and cries and says you've lost your mind and that we have to find some way to save you."

"What do you tell her?"

"I don't tell her anything. Candy just tells her she's right and that she's lucky to be shut of you."

"Do you think I've lost my mind?"

"Maybe so. Maybe a little."

I thought it over. "No," I said. "I feel sane enough."

"What is this place you're going to, anyway?"

"I don't know a thing about it," I confessed. "It's called Beaufort. It's across the lake."

"Well, I wish you good luck, old boy," he said, staring into the triangular opening of his beer can. "Just real good luck." We worked until midnight and succeeded in pushing my possessions into a pile in the center of the living room. David had his books, a lamp, and a bedside table set to one side. We decided to dump the heavy things that were in the truck directly after work, then return for a second load. We settled ourselves on the front stairs again for our final beer. David leaned back and gazed up into the heavens, full of good fellowship. "What a night," he said softly.

I watched a streetcar lurching around the corner at Carrollton, hurtling toward us in the darkness, bereft of passengers. Another streetcar appeared from the opposite direction, rocking along sleepily, its driver in no hurry. The two converged on one another before us and the one on the far side stopped, its brakes whining. For a moment I was dazzled by the lights from the cars, the eerie silhouette of the drivers, the strangely familiar back of the passenger who was swinging down to the pavement. Then the cars parted and Alex stood hesitantly between the still-singing tracks.

"Christ," I said when I recognized her. She was looking from one side of the street to the other, trying to make out the addresses. I jumped up and went to her. "Alex," I called.

She turned to me, smiling, pleased with herself. "Look at that," she said. "I found you first try."

I embraced her briefly on the neutral ground and led her to where David sat wide-eyed and dumb on the stairs.

It was exactly what I hadn't wanted to happen. I didn't want her to know any of my friends but particularly David, who, though he is kind, generous, and full of unsuspected sensibilities (his love of opera, his mania for Buñuel films), has the deadening air of the overworked, familied, worried, and balding accountant he is. And I didn't want Alex to see my apartment ever, for reasons that are, at this point, obvious.

She was in high spirits, I could feel it through the cloth of her blouse. She had given her notice at the bar and had an argument with the owner which resulted in her walking out that very night, swearing never to return. Then she had traced me through the phone book and come up to see what I was doing. She knew that I wouldn't be leaving to meet her for another hour but still she had feared she might have missed me, or might cross cars with me on the way. She told me all this in a rush and finished by holding her hand out genially to David, who stood up confusedly and took her hand in his own as if he meant to keep it. I introduced them. They stood hand in hand, friendly, both curiously excited, and I realized with a thud in my heart and a flash of pain in my jaw that I didn't want another man to touch her. David released her and stumbled on the step, trying to retrieve his beer. Alex flashed me an amazed look. How my friend was amusing her!

David got to his feet and said he was just leaving, he really had to go. "It's nice to meet you," he added. "I've heard so much about you."

Alex let the remark pass, a bit of graciousness I didn't expect. "We could all go out together," she suggested. "We could go right over there." She pointed to the bar and restaurant across the street. "I'm starved, anyway."

David reiterated his parting remarks and bowing and shuffling made his way down the stairs and out to his truck. I asked Alex to wait a moment and followed him. "I'll see you tomorrow," I said.

"Great. Sure," he replied.

I felt hateful in spite of his innocence. "Well now you've had your wish," I said. "You've seen her."

And that was when he made that stupid remark I mentioned earlier—"a little masculine, but nice"—which irritated me even more when he drove away and I turned to find Alex sitting on the stair drinking the remains of my beer, her legs apart, her boots planted squarely on the next step down, like a cowboy relaxing after a roundup. I sat down beside her.

"What's the matter," she said. "You didn't want me to come here?"

"The place is a wreck," I said. "I'm trying to get rid of everything by Friday."

"I don't care about that," she said. "I thought it would be nice for a change." She paused. "My coming to you, I mean."

"You're hungry," I said. "Let's go get something to eat."

We went to the restaurant across the street and I watched her devour a large plate of spaghetti and meatballs, French bread, salad, and two beers. She ate without talking, hurriedly, as if someone might take the plate away from her. When she was finished she leaned back in her chair and wiped her mouth delicately with the napkin, then ordered coffee. "I ought to warn you," she said. "We won't get any meat at Beaufort."

"Why not?"

"Diana's a vegetarian."

I didn't care, have never cared much what I eat. "That's okay with me," I said.

"I still can't believe it," she said. "I can't believe you're really coming with me."

"Have you changed your mind?"

She ladled two spoons of sugar into her coffee. "Never," she said, sipping it and giving me an inviting look over the rim of the cup. "Not for a minute."

We went back to my apartment. She didn't stop in the doorway as I had imagined she might, dismayed and disgusted. Instead, she strolled into the mess without looking at it, shoved a pile of pots off the mattress (the bed was in David's truck), and made herself comfortable. "You got any more beer?" she asked.

I took two beers from the icebox and sat down beside her. "It doesn't seem right, seeing you here," I said.

"If you think this is strange, wait until tomorrow. I'm going to stick around and get a look at you in the cold light of day."

I nodded, unable to think of anything to say. The notion that I had given up my freedom completely, that my time was hers now, my will hers, my imagination hers, that I was no longer my own man (had I ever been?), dawned on me and chilled me. But I dismissed it. How could that be when my will was to be with her? Just to watch her; I desired nothing more. She lay on her side, propped up on one elbow, sipping her beer and gazing vacantly out into space. If I stayed with her every day for the next six months, as I planned, would I be able to read that expression and know her thoughts? Or would she remain as mysterious, as otherworldly, would her manner be as recondite, her smile as undecipherable? I reached out and pushed her hair back over one shoulder, then touched her cheek with the palm of my hand. Her eyes settled on me reluctantly. "We'll be seeing a lot of each other now," she said. She set her beer can on the floor and turned to me, her lips already parted and her eyes half closed, reaching for me languidly and pulling me down.

5

When I woke, the sun was streaming through my worn curtains and Alex was asleep at my side. Or rather, below my side, for she had rolled off the mattress and lay in a nest of sheets on the floor. I got up quietly, brushed my teeth, arranged my sleep-shocked hair, and put water on to boil in the kitchen. Then I stood in the doorway looking at Alex.

She lay on her stomach, her face turned toward me, her arms stretched out as if reaching for me. Her mouth was slightly open and a stray lock of hair covered one eye and darkened the hollow of her cheek. Her breathing was shallow and slow—I could discern it only in the cleft of her breasts, pressed together interestingly by the weight of her arm. Her face, her posture, the glow of her skin, even the sheen of her hair, created an impression of such delicate beauty, such innocence, that I was awed by the sight. As I watched, her eyes opened, blinked, opened wide, and her face was flushed with busy intelligence, transforming her in a way that saddened even as it excited me. She looked about the room quickly, then turned over on her back and her eyes came to rest upon me.

"You're up."

"I was watching you sleep," I said, turning away. The water was boiling and I measured out coffee into the pot. Alex got up and followed me to the kitchen. She put her arms around my waist and rubbed her cheek against my back, slowly, sleepily, but I felt aloof and didn't turn to her. After a moment she released me and I heard her close the bathroom door. Then I heard water running in the sink.

I poured water over the coffee grounds and tried to concentrate on my plans for the day. I would need a suitcase by Friday and it might be necessary to purchase some new clothing. I wondered how one dressed at Beaufort. Through my speculations there glimmered a pale line of doubt, like the dull silver edge of waves on a dark night. It was something about Alex, something unpronounced, unconscious. She was nervous, I thought, and why shouldn't she be. I poured coffee into two cups. Alex came out of the bathroom and resumed her place on the floor, pulling a brush through her long hair. I brought her cup to her and sat near her, in a straight-back chair.

"I've got to buy a suitcase today," she said.

"I was thinking the same thing."

She turned to look at me. "I'll get you one when I get mine. How big do you want it?"

"I don't know. How much should I bring?"

"Not much. Jeans. Shirts. Sweaters. We won't need anything else." She eyed my shoes, which were toe to toe at the foot of the mattress. "You might want different shoes for walking."

"I won't have time to buy all that."

"Just give me some money and your sizes and I'll get everything you need," she said.

I accepted this offer. I wrote my sizes down on the back of an envelope and put a check for $500, made out to her, inside. She took it out and didn't seem surprised at the amount. She laughed when she saw that I had used her full name. "Alexandra," she said. "No one calls me that."

She turned over on her stomach and rifled the sheets looking for her clothes, then spotted her shirt near the wall. There was a small box next to it, containing the few objects I wished to keep, and Alex saw the photograph on top. "Who's that?" she said, pointing to it.

I looked at the picture, which was upside down so that the woman's shy smile was a frown and her eyes seemed to be looking down at me. "My mother," I said.

Alex got up and pulled the picture to her, sitting cross-legged on the mattress with my mother's face smiling sadly up at her from her lap. "Is she alive?"

"No. She died when I was thirteen."

"Oh," she said. She returned the picture to its box and retrieved her shirt. "Who raised you?" she asked.

"My grandmother."

She had the shirt on and was busily pulling on her underpants. "That's really strange," she said. "I was raised by an aunt."

"Your mother died?"

"No," she said. "Actually, I don't know what happened to her. She left me with my aunt when I was a baby."

She stood up and stepped into her jeans. "What kind of suitcase do you want?" she asked.

"I don't care," I said. I was swamped with images and in the wake of them I experienced the particular torture of my consciousness, the total inability to concentrate on anything. I picked my cup up from the floor and put it down again. Alex stood, idly watching me. I was thinking of my mother, of the paltry, thin, colorless memories I have of her, of the face I know only from a picture, and of Alex, as she might have been at three, at ten, at twenty, left to shift steadfastly for herself, and of myself at thirteen, standing amid my indifferent relatives in the clear, hot, buzzing August air, the toes of my shoes turned in to avoid touching the edge of the hole they had dug for my mother, my eyes riveted upon a large black beetle skittering frantically toward the wall of that hole as the coffin blackened his sky and descended, creaking and swaying, to crush him.

"Come on," Alex said. "Do you want an expensive one or a cheap one?"

"Expensive," I said.

She looked around at the room, then sat on the floor to put her boots on. I was still too absorbed in my thoughts. My feet were asleep and I recalled an account I'd read by a man who had come back to life after being dead a record length of time, ten minutes, five minutes, I couldn't remember. He said his death had started in his feet and moved up.

"This place is a wreck," Alex said, standing up again. She stood near me, folding the envelope with my check in it and shoving it down into her pocket. I looked up into her wide solemn eyes. There were grainy dark circles beneath them and the palpebral skin was reticulated with blue veins, blood moving through invisible veins even as I watched. We shared a long sad look, like comrades about to leave the safety of their foxhole to make a run for their lives.

"I guess I'd better get started," she said. "Should I come back here this evening?"

"I'm just going to be packing."

"I've got some things to do at my place. I'll come back late. After midnight."

"Okay," I said. This relieved me because it meant she would miss David. I got up and began looking around for my pants. Alex stood smiling in the doorway, then, when I turned away, she left. I crossed the room and closed the door.

I had to go to work. In four more days my job would be over forever but I felt that it was too long to wait. I wanted to be done with it at once. I was aggravated, my stomach burned and my head ached. I decided to have breakfast across the street and read the paper slowly. Alex was everywhere in my thoughts, like a shadow, something moving in the corner of my view, something sudden and heart-stopping, and every time I came across her I was surprised to find that it was only her. I dressed quickly and left the apartment, slamming the door behind me.

I worked at my desk all day, drinking several cups of coffee and eating a sandwich David brought me. I threw out great baskets of paper and filed another stack haphazardly and hurriedly. My supervisor came by and attempted for a few minutes to understand my system. Then he sent a secretary to assist me.

I did not wonder who my replacement would be because I knew. He was a young, colorless computer programmer who would spend three weeks over my work, the scribbled figures of twenty-five years. He would crack my system one morning after his tenth cup of coffee and translate the whole mess into the government's fine new computer, which was full of empty memory banks just waiting for someone to quit so it could digest a lifetime of figures. After that my job would be done by this nifty machine. I wished it luck. My secretary, the matronly Miss Babar, who had worked for the government even longer than I, soon convinced me that most of the stuff I was filing should be thrown away and that much of the stuff I was throwing out would prove indispensable to the young computer programmer. We began anew. By four-thirty I was tired, as was Miss Babar, and we cleared a small section of the desk for two cups of coffee. Miss Babar produced from her purse a fragrant tangerine, which she divided neatly in half, offering to share with me. I accepted.

"Your termination is rather sudden, isn't it?" she inquired, gracefully sucking the end of a tangerine slice.

"My termination is extremely sudden," I said. "Also extremely overdue."

Miss Babar sipped her coffee. "Then you have been contemplating it for some time."

"I have, indeed," I lied.

Miss Babar indicated the room with a lift of her chin. "Who among us has not?" she concluded.

63

I smiled at Miss Babar and wondered why we had never shared a tangerine before. She ate two more slices, delicately sucking her fingertips after each. Then she gave me her full attention. "They tell me," she said, "that you're running away with a young woman."

"Yes, I am," I said. I didn't have to guess how she had got this information and resolved that David would regret our next meeting.

"Well," she said. "You are the sort of man who must do that sort of thing, I suppose." Then she placed her tangerine peel in a Kleenex and deposited it in my trash can. "I hope it goes well for you," she said. "I'll just wash these cups out." She left my desk.

I sat amid the rubble and thought that no matter how I tried I would never see myself as others saw me. Miss Babar had been watching me for years and she thought she knew me. At Beaufort, I thought, I would not have to endure the scrutiny of anyone who knew me. I would be an unknown man. I was eager to go. The three days I had left would be intolerable.

But, because there was so much to be done, those days passed quickly. By Friday my apartment was empty, my new clothes (Alex had decided to re-do me from top to bottom. I had new shoes, socks, pants, shirts, one sweater, all in brown, black, or white) were packed away in my new elegant brown leather suitcase that matched Alex's boots. She arrived at my apartment at five-thirty, her luggage in hand. This consisted of one wicker suitcase, light and practical, and a small alligator case with a bone handle, clearly designed to hold something specific.

"What's in there?" I asked when she set this case down next to mine.

"My knives," she said.

"Knives?" I eyed the case.

"Open it," she said. "It's not locked."

I opened the case and there, resting in velvet with purple

velvet sheaths over the blades, were five knives. I removed one and pulled off the sheath. The handle was wooden, dark, and polished, with a gold stud set in the end. The blade was oiled, brilliant, sharp, and curiously shaped; a long triangle coming to a needle point about a foot from the base. When I placed this base against my thumb the knife balanced perfectly, dipping slightly back and forth like a scale. "What are they for?" I asked.

"They're for throwing," she said. "Like in the circus. It's my hobby."

"Are you any good at it?" I took the knife from my thumb and slipped it back into its sheath.

"I am excellent at it," she said.

I held the knife out to her, handle first. "Would you demonstrate?"

She took it from me and returned it to its case. "Not now," she said. "I'll show you at Beaufort. We've got half an hour to get to the lake. Diana is punctual."

I looked around at my empty apartment. The mattress, which I was leaving, lay in the center of the room. The rest was dust and emptiness. The sun streamed through the uncurtained windows, and the floor, without its worn rugs, was shiny in spots. Alex had picked up her bag and stood at the door. "Let's go," she said. I followed her out to the street.

We took a streetcar to the end of the line on Carrollton, a bus from there to Canal Street, and another bus to Lake Pontchartrain. We got off at the marina and stood on the curb blinking at each other in the glare of the afternoon sun. "Is she coming in here?" I asked Alex.

"No," she said. "We have to walk out to the fishing pier. There's a slip there where she can get us without coming into the harbor."

"Will she stop," I asked, "or will we have to swim out to her?"

Alex shrugged. "It's the way she always does it."

We walked along past the marina, down a shady oystershell road and out past a long row of boathouses. A few of these houses were rusting sheds but most were freshly painted, with sparkling windows and a deck tacked on over the front, invariably scattered with lawn chairs and red wood tables. I felt conspicuous walking along with my suitcase. Occasionally a boat owner glided by in a big car or glowered down at us from a deck, drink in hand. Alex was indifferent, she walked quickly and purposefully. We came to the fishing pier, a wooden deck jutting out over the water, and walked down a tangled path behind it that led to a most rudimentary dock. There was a narrow wooden platform and an old gas pump surrounded by crushed beer cans. We slid down a slight embankment and went out to the platform. "What time is it?" Alex asked.

I looked at my watch. "Ten to six," I said.

She put her bag down but retained her knife case. "We've got ten minutes," she said. "You want to sit down?"

I didn't. I looked out over the water and saw a sailboat coming our way. The crew was busy, pulling lines and running around on the deck. I know nothing about sailing and their efforts seemed disproportionate to the ease with which the bow of their craft riffled the calm water. The sun was behind the boat, washing it in soft refracted light so that it looked like a line drawing filled in with pastels. There was an opacity to the air that pleased me; it was cool, distant, salt-laden, wet, easy to breathe. I breathed in deeply, feeling lighthearted. I was not thinking of Diana.

Alex stood beside me, fidgeting with the handle of her knife case, changing feet, leaning against the gas pump, kicking at the beer cans. Every minute she gave the water a long worried look, squinting at the sun. I followed her gaze a few times but couldn't see what she was looking at. After a few minutes she said, "There she is."

I followed her eyes and this time I saw a small triangle of white moving toward us across the water. It was far away, much too far to make out distinctly, and I wondered what made Alex sure it was Diana. Alex's gaze was riveted to the triangle from then on. She watched it grow and I watched her become increasingly agitated as it did so. Her hands left a wet mark on the knife case when she moved it from one side to the other. The light creases in her forehead grew deeper and deeper, then flattened out abruptly as she noticed that I was watching her.

"You're sure that's her?" I asked.

"What?" she said. "Yes, I'm sure."

Then I watched the triangle. It was more than that now; the hull was visible and could be distinguished from the lower and upper decks. The boat sped toward us, then turned abruptly so that I could see its long profile. It was a large motorboat with a closed cabin below and an open, glass-fronted bridge above, all white with chrome trim, modern, powerful, and sleek. It was moving at such speed that the hull was lifted from the water. I could make out a woman dressed in white standing at the wheel on the upper deck. I couldn't see her face or determine much about her figure. I looked at Alex, who stood clutching her knife case against her chest with one hand, holding her suitcase in the other. I couldn't read the expression on her face, except to see that it contained a complex of emotions. She looked at me, smiled wanly, and looked back at the boat.

We could hear the motor clearly then and as it approached us the volume was suddenly cut in half and the boat's speed slowed correspondingly. I could see Diana more clearly and what I saw made me smile with admiration. As she floated toward me across the water the sun met the horizon and bled the sky behind her red and ocher. She was bigger than life, more disturbing than a dream. She held the wheel expertly in her hands and steered steadily toward us. Gradually I became aware of her eyes upon me. I was also able to get some idea of her real size and it unsettled me. She was well over six feet tall and the fluttering folds of her dress did not conceal the remarkable swelling of her belly. I felt her eyes leave my face and I was able to look at hers. In that light, her face becoming steadily more real, more distinct, confused me. There was no mistaking the sensuality of her full mouth. The bones of her cheeks were high and visible, distracting from her mouth and giving her a fashion model's hollowness. Her hair, long, wild, blond, blowing about her face in a fury, drew my attention to her eyes, which were immediately fastened upon my own with such determination that I looked away.

The boat was very close then and I was able to see two big dogs pacing about in the open back of the lower deck. She cut the motor completely and drifted closer and closer. Alex put her bags down and went to the edge of the dock, holding out her hands to catch the rope Diana threw down to her. I stood back, enjoying the sight of the two women securing the boat expertly and easily, without speaking. The dogs were barking and whining and Alex yelled at one, "Be still. I'm coming." I came forward and stood behind Alex, feeling as awkward as I have ever felt. I realized that I didn't even know if Alex had mentioned me to Diana. "Can I do anything?" I said.

Alex gave me a harried look. "You can get on now." I looked at the dogs, who were eyeing me, slobbering and baring their teeth but, I noticed, wagging their tails at the same time. "You get on first," I said. "I'll get this rope."

This pleased her and she moved down the dock, handing our luggage to Diana, who leaned out over the water precariously. Alex leaped aboard and the two women embraced quickly, impersonally. I heard Alex say, "Diana," her voice soft and affectionate. Then they separated and Alex gestured to Diana's great stomach. "You're far gone," she said.

Diana laughed and patted herself. I busied myself untying the rope Alex had secured and pulling it along toward the back of the boat. The boat began to drift away alarmingly. "Are you afraid of dogs?" Alex yelled to me.

"No," I said. I gave the rope a tug, causing the bow to

turn in to me and the side to drift farther away. I was aware of a hand stretching out to me across the widening strip of water and I reached for it, leaping spectacularly from the dock, rope in hand, heart in throat. My new soft-soled shoes hit and gripped the edge of the boat and I fell into it, greeted by exclamations, barking, big dog feet, slapping tails, and wet tongues. I sat up on the floor and looked around cheerfully. The two women bent over me, anxious to get me on my feet. I had made my leap of faith.

I got up without assistance and brushed myself off. Alex introduced me to Diana, who held out her hand to me. I took it in my own, surprised by the firmness of her grip. "I've leaped into your boat," I said, looking for the first time into her eyes.

She was smiling, looking down at me from her superior vantage, her eyes a little sleepy, distant, but at the same time as deep and as mad as a trapped animal.

"Most imprudent of you," she said. She ushered us into the lower cabin, shoving the dogs aside with her knee. I grabbed the suitcases and followed Alex in. "I'll go up now," Diana said, closing the door behind us. She disappeared up a narrow flight of steps and I heard the motor speed up a moment later.

"Well," I said to Alex. "How long does it take?"

She was sitting at a built-in table, leaning out of her seat to open a small refrigerator across from her. "About an hour," she said. "Do you want a beer? Or Scotch?"

"Beer," I said, taking a place at the table. The motor grew louder and the boat began to pull away from the dock.

"What do you think of her?" Alex asked, setting a beer in front of me. It was Bass ale, a brand I am fond of but rarely bought because it is too expensive.

"She's impressive," I said.

"Does she seem strange to you?"

"In what way?"

"Nothing," she said. "Never mind." She stretched her legs out and rested her head against the back of her seat. I sipped my beer.

"Who is the father of that bulge?" I asked.

"I don't know much about him. He's an Italian and he's short."

"How short?"

"I don't know. Shorter than me."

"What are his feelings about the child?"

"He'd marry Diana if he could."

"But she won't?"

"No." Alex opened a drawer in the table and took out a deck of cards. "She won't. You want to play cards?"

I nodded. Outside our sealed glass compartment the shoreline was slipping away. We played one hand of gin, which Alex won, and when I looked up there was only a smudgy line of black where the dock had been. One of the dogs had settled down outside our door, lying on his side beneath a seat at the back of the boat. I couldn't see the other. We finished our beers and started new ones. Alex threw the empty cans into a built-in trash bin that pulled out of the cabin wall. I looked around carefully and noted the number of conveniences that could be used for storage, cooking, and disposing. "You could live here," I remarked.

Alex put her beer can into a swinging holder next to the table. Another holder swung empty next to me and I examined it, then put my half-full can into it and watched it sway back and forth, not spilling a drop. When I looked at Alex she was grinning broadly.

"What's funny?" I said.

"You like gadgets?" she inquired rhetorically.

"I've never been in a boat like this. You seem familiar with it."

"I am," she said. "I used to spend a lot of time on it."

"It's nice," I said. "Everything is designed for convenience and comfort."

She nodded at me, amused.

"Is Beaufort like this?" I asked.

She gave me a mischievous smile. "There's something I didn't tell you about Beaufort," she said.

"You didn't tell me anything. But what is it?"

"Beaufort," she said, holding out her beer can in the direction of our motion, "is paradise."

I followed her gesture and looked out over the water at the approaching shore. Already I could make out sand, a line of green trees, and above it I contemplated uncertainly a darkening sky, curving over the shoreline like a dome and containing both the last burning streaks of the dying sun and the pale phantom crescent of a new and vaporous moon.

6

It was dark by the time we reached the other shore. Diana steered us along the beach for a way, then turned into a wide bayou that led farther north. It got darker still. Cypress trees lined the banks and their limbs hung out over the water, trailing long fingers of moss and ivy. The bayou narrowed, turned, forked, and the boat moved slowly through the water. I drank another beer and looked out the window, feeling drowsy but apprehensive.

We passed a row of houses, modern brick and glass constructions with landscaped grounds curving down to boat slips that looked as if they had been cut out of the bank with a stamp. There was a country-club house on our left—a colonial edifice with two unseemly Victorian turrets and a wide porch all round scattered with deck chairs. The bayou curved and for a while there was nothing but the most impenetrable jungle, black and deep, revealed in sudden intimate patches by the headlights of the boat. We passed a few small houses, fishing camps, built down close to the water. Then the bayou grew wider and we entered another long section of dense jungle.

"This is Beaufort's land," Alex said. She had pressed her cheek against the windowpane and she looked pensively at the smudged glass. She smiled at me and I leaned across the table to kiss her. Then she returned her attention to the window. "There's the house," she said.

I looked up and saw, not the house, but a moss-laden limb of cypress hanging down over the boat, and from it, the long shiny coil of a water snake slithering down to the black water. Then the limb was gone and I was looking across a wide formal garden laid out like two hands pointing their thumbs at the house. The house was large and so brightly lit that it looked as though it were blazing, sending up streams of dusty light into the dark and fragrant air. Our boat hummed, turning into the slip, then the motor was quiet. Alex jumped up, stashing our beer cans in the waste bin and emptying the ashtrays as well.

"You are the neatest woman I've ever met," I observed.

"It's a habit," she said. "Let's go."

As I got up I saw Diana coming down from the flying bridge, first her feet in their flat soft-soled shoes, then her slender ankles, her long calves, the edge of her skirt filling out like a sail over her large stomach, her full breasts, shoulders, light hair, and suddenly her white, damp face. She turned toward us and opened the door to the cabin. The dogs were up, pushing about on the deck. Alex threw a line over a cleat and Diana spoke to the dogs. "Go on," she said. "You can go now."

They leaped from the boat and ran wildly for the house, barking and falling headlong over the dark shrubbery. As I watched, the front door of the house opened and a woman stood in the frame. "That's Collie," Alex said, noting my gaze. She jumped onto the dock and caught the rope Diana threw her. I followed, bringing the rope from the stern with me. When the boat was fastened we walked up to the house, Diana leading and Alex and I behind. I took Alex's hand in my own and she pressed it warmly, then moved close to me so that I would put my arm around her. At the door she stepped away and embraced the woman, who, I noted with mild surprise, was a Negro. Her skin was a luminous bronze in the porch light and her wide brown eyes, which regarded me coolly over Alex's white shoulder, were tilted up at the corners like an Oriental's. She held Alex tightly, then released her. "Girl," she said. "You stay away too long." Alex turned to me and introduced us. I took Collie's hand but it was limp and cool and she acknowledged me only by nodding her head in my direction.

We went inside. Diana had disappeared and I followed Alex, who turned into the first room and threw herself down in a stuffed chair as if she were exhausted from great activity. Collie looked in the door and said, "Dinner in fifteen minutes." Then she, too, disappeared down the hall.

I took a chair near Alex and looked around the room. It was comfortably furnished with large tufted leather chairs and a number of small tables. The walls were lined with shelves of books. Later I learned the rest of the house and found it all to my liking. Beaufort has sixteen rooms, eight downstairs, eight up. It is divided by a central hall on both floors and the rooms all open onto this hall as well as onto each other. A wide veranda surrounds the lower floor and each room has French doors that open onto it. This means that there are four doors in every room, though, for the most part, the doors that connect the rooms aren't used. All the furnishings are plain, expensive, comfortable, and it would be hard to identify the style of the decoration. There is a good deal of velvet and oak and there are elegant thick carpets everywhere. The floors that show at their edges are of polished cypress. The room Alex and I sat in that first night is the library. I strained my eyes to read some of the book titles and absently pressed the toe of my shoe into the carpet. Alex sank down in her chair, her chin upon her breastbone. She looked up at me. "What do you think?" she said.

"I'm interested."

She laughed. "I'll bet you are."

My stomach growled audibly. "I'm hungry, too," I said.

"It won't be long." She jumped out of her chair and went to a squat liquor cabinet that crouched in a corner like a frog. She poured herself a small glass of something. "You want brandy?" she asked.

"No thank you," I said, examining a section of the books. I noted a new set of encyclopedias and several volumes of C. S. Lewis stuffed in between *The Monk* and *Elmer Gantry*, the former clearly misfiled. "Does Diana read a lot?"

Alex pursed her lips. "She reads, dances, rides horses, water-skis, and . . ." There was suddenly the sound of a piano, the first chords of Beethoven's "Pathétique," followed by a rapid flood of scales from one end of the keyboard to the other. "And plays the piano," Alex concluded. She stood next to me, sipping her brandy. "She can do anything," she said.

"I see," I said, turning to her. She gave me a look of exultation that surprised me; she looked as if she had caught me in a trap. The scales had turned back into Beethoven, the adagio now, and the music drifted to us through the air like a perfume. I wanted to kiss Alex and looked over her shoulder at an inviting couch on which I quickly imagined a scene of hurried passion, but I could feel a chill coming from her, as if she were growing stiff at the sight of me, and I thought it best to walk away. I went to the door and looked down the empty hall. "She plays very well," I said.

Alex shrugged and went back to her chair. "I'm glad you think so," she said petulantly, "because she plays all the time." I remained in the doorway for a few moments. Alex said, "Let's go eat," and passed through the door without touching me. I followed her down the hall.

The dining room was the third door on the left. It was brightly lit by a massive chandelier, thick with prisms and dazzling with light. The table was set with china and crystal and there were four places. The room opened onto the kitchen, where we could hear the sounds of an electric mixer. Alex went into the kitchen and came back a moment later carrying a plate upon which raw vegetables made a nimbostratus around a bowl of sour cream. She held it out to me and I took a slice of carrot and another of celery.

Then she opened the doors to the porch and there was a rush of damp warm air ushered in by the faint whirr of the ceiling fans. I heard a high-pitched tinkling, a thin glassy sound that could be heard over all the others, like the triangle in a symphony orchestra. The piano music stopped and a moment later Diana appeared at the door. She smiled at Alex and indicated me with a lift of her chin. "You know who he looks like," she said. Alex scowled.

"Who?" I said to Diana.

"Someone from our past," Diana replied.

"Someone dead," Alex added. Collie came from the kitchen carrying a serving dish heaped with steaming vegetables. Diana began pouring wine from a decanter into the glasses and Alex followed Collie back into the kitchen. "You can pour the water," Diana said.

I did as she suggested. "I hope you'll be comfortable here," she continued. "If anything doesn't suit you, I hope you'll feel free to tell me."

I watched the water flowing from the silver pitcher in my hand to the crystal glass beneath. It was slightly carbonated and so clear it made me salivate to look at it. Then I looked up at Diana. She had finished her task and was pressing the stopper back into the decanter. Her eyes, however, were on me, wide and strange, and the corners of her mouth were quivering with suppressed laughter.

"Do I amuse you?" I asked.

"I think you will," she said.

I gave her what I imagined was a look of cool speculation. Alex and Collie returned from the kitchen loaded with

77

dishes. There was a platter of rice and another of steamed rolls, a clover dish containing three sauces, a divided bowl heaped with grated cheeses, a small dish of mushrooms in brown gravy, and a tureen of thick pale soup that turned out to be concocted from lettuce and carrots. The women arranged these dishes on the table and took their seats, Diana at the head, Collie and Alex facing each other at her side. I took the remaining chair next to Alex.

We occupied ourselves for a few moments passing dishes around and piling our plates with food. Diana looked from one of us to the other, her eyes glittering with amusement. She dipped her spoon into her soup and sipped it cautiously. "Perfect," she said to Collie.

Alex ate with her usual abandon and looked up only to smile at me. I began tasting the hill of food on my plate and was surprised to find how good everything was. From outdoors we could hear the whirr of the fans and the desultory singing of a night bird. Diana put down her spoon. "How strange," she said, "for us to be together again."

Collie nodded. "It is strange," she said. "Why were we ever separated?"

"I don't know," Diana said. "How could we have let it happen?" She paused, gazing vacantly at Alex. "Do you know?" she asked.

Alex gave her a sullen look. "You know I'm not very good at reminiscing," she said.

Diana laughed. "I know you think it's a waste of time."

"That, too," Alex replied.

Diana grew serious. "Do you wish you hadn't come?"

"No," Alex said. She tapped a snowy napkin against her lips. "I wanted to come."

"But you wouldn't have if you hadn't been able to persuade Claude to come with you."

Alex shrugged and reached for her glass.

"Which is why I count you so dear," she said, turning to me.

Later, when we sat alone together on the porch, drinking brandy and coffee and listening to the combined music of Diana's piano and Collie's clattering dishes, I asked Alex if this was true.

"I wouldn't have come without you," she said. "I couldn't have."

"But why?" I persisted.

She gave me a maddening smile. "You're my offering," she said.

Later still, after several glasses of brandy and the descent of a considerable stupor over my faculties, I was shown to my room by the indifferent Collie. She indicated the door which connects Alex's room to mine, and the other door, which, she said, led to my bath. Then she left me and I stood gazing out the window, down into the top of a palm tree that leaned its heavy head toward the house like an intruder. There was a knock at my door.

"Come in," I said.

Alex came in, reeling under the influence of the two glasses of brandy she had on me. She ran her fingertip over the leather inset of the writing desk, then perched awkwardly on the end of the bed. "How do you like your room?" she asked.

I looked around. I've since come to love it, but it is decorated with some other gentleman in mind, one more accustomed to luxury than I. "It's swell," I said.

She laughed. "Before you come over here I want to make a quick deal."

"What's that?"

She pointed to our adjoining door. "We'll always knock before entering and you'll not be offended if I tell you to go away."

"And if I tell *you* to go away?"

She pouted. "You noticed that part, huh?" She tried to prop her elbows on her knees but one slipped off and she nearly fell from the bed. I watched her, amused by the speed with which she regained her composure, accomplished the posture she had been trying for, then abandoned it and threw herself back on the bed. Her long calves in their smooth boots hung over the edge of the bed.

"I'll take your boots off," I said.

She sighed. "Please."

I pulled a chair from the desk and sat down, propping her foot in my lap. She lay quietly, her arms thrown out over her head, gazing at the ceiling. I thought her very lovely and I was anxious to get the boots off and proceed to the rest, but at the same time I was annoyed with her. I felt she knew that my desire for her drove me to extremes I might otherwise despise. I pulled the boots off roughly and threw them against the wall. She watched me, lazy, smiling, encouraging me. I unfastened her jeans and pulled them open and down over her hips. She lifted her hips to help me but her effort was slight, casual. Her eyes were half closed and the dull expression on her face made me want to shake her. I kissed her, forcing her mouth open and bruising her soft lips with my teeth. When I let her go she looked up at me, smiling sleepily. "How can you be angry with me?" she said, brushing my mouth with her fingertips.

In the past I had been careful never to hurt her, never to brace my arm across her chest or push her back into too deep a curve or pin her head uncomfortably beneath me, but this time I didn't care and thought, as I hooked her legs over my elbows, if I hurt her she would let me know. I treated her roughly, biting her, tearing at her, and dragging her about so viciously I thought I must pull her apart. She was quiet and yielding, encouraging me with sighs, flinching occasionally, but uncomplaining. When I was done I rolled away from her and said, "What a strong girl you are."

She laughed. "One day you're going to kill yourself doing that," she said.

We lay still for a while and I began to drift off to sleep. I felt the bed move as she got up, searching the bed for her pants, leaning over me so that I felt her soft breath on my side. Then I heard the door between our rooms open and close and I knew I was alone.

It was quiet. I opened my eyes and lay looking into the darkness, pleasantly tired and comfortable. The windows in my room were open and I could hear the soft rustling of the leaves outside. It was a warm night but I was cool and I decided to pull back the heavy velvet spread and lie beneath the sheets. These turned out to be satin, cool and smooth against my skin. I wished for Alex but gradually the comfort of being able to spread myself out, legs apart, arms out at my sides, made me feel that it was better to be alone. I imagined that I had fallen from a plane and landed in the luxurious lap of a towering goddess, a notion that made me smile. Then I heard the sound of the piano, soft at first, swelling a little, a slow and languorous song such as a woman might sing over a sleeping child. I closed my eyes and let the music pour over me and it seemed the air had turned to liquid and I was floating upon it. I imagined Diana sitting at the piano, her arms raised over her big stomach, her hair pushed back behind her delicate ears, her wild eyes closed as she filled the house with music so rich and sad it seemed to lift us all from the earth's dark surface. A feeling of giddiness swept over me and I opened my eyes, thinking at first that I saw a light in the darkness around me. But there was nothing. My heart felt light, fluttering, missing a beat, then doubling up on the next. I put my hand over my chest and pressed against it, my sturdy reliable heart. "Something will happen to me," I said, surprised myself to hear my voice in the dark room. The music stopped abruptly. A few moments later I heard footsteps on the stairs, along the hall, passing my door and stopping at the end of the hall. There was a flash of light beneath my door, narrowing to a thin line as Diana closed the door of her room behind her. Then the house was still, silent, heavy with sleep, and I lay gazing into the darkness for a long time before my thoughts became confused and I fell into a dream.

In the morning I woke to find a few dull rays of light scattered through the curtains. The house was quiet but I could smell coffee and since I couldn't find a clock in my room I got dressed and went downstairs. I had slept well and was in a good humor, in spite of my discovery that it was cloudy and threatened rain outdoors. I followed my nose to the kitchen, where I found Collie turning the pages of a newspaper while she sipped coffee and chewed on a hard roll. She looked up at me and smiled, more cordial than the night before. "You the first one up," she said.

"You don't count yourself?" I said.

She got up and went to the stove. "Sit down," she said. "I'll bring you your coffee. You can have some of these rolls or you can wait till the others come down. I'll fix some eggs and grits then."

I sat at the table and helped myself to a roll, which proved to be full of chopped dates. "Do you make these rolls?" I asked, chewing.

"I make all the food," she said. "It's my job."

It had not occurred to me that she might be in Diana's employ. She didn't appear to be a servant. The possibility intrigued me and I wanted to ask her, but feared that if she wasn't a servant she might be insulted by the idea. I sipped the strong coffee she put before me and decided on a new tack. I had plenty of questions. "Would you tell me something?" I asked.

"I could tell you a lot. You look like you need to know it."

"I'm not certain how I fit in here," I admitted.

She shrugged, a mannerism that made me think of Alex. "We need a man."

"Who is it," I said, "that I remind Diana of?"

"That's a long story."

"I'd like to hear it."

She stirred her coffee and looked into its swirling surface. "Why don't you ask Alex?" she said.

"She would think I was prying."

She laughed. "You're a smart man, after all. You're on to Alex already."

"So you'll tell me," I insisted.

"Sure," she said. "Sure, why not?"

7

Collie folded her paper in half and pushed it out of sight between two counters. It was, I later learned, an old paper which she read over and over. Diana didn't allow any news at Beaufort. She refilled her cup and stirred sugar into it, composing her thoughts. "Diana and Alex and I grew up in the same house together," she said. "But we all knew it was Diana's house."

"I don't understand," I said.

"It was because of Miss Laura, Diana's mother. She was a rich woman even before she married Mr. Laurentis. She was headstrong and had odd ideas about a lot of things. She wouldn't have a servant unless she housed him at the place where he worked, and she knew about all the affairs of the people that worked for her. She kept a big staff, most people thought it was bigger than she needed.

"She had a white woman that worked for her, I think she called her her secretary, but what she did nobody could ever figure out. Miss Laura was fond of her and gave her three rooms in the big town house all to herself. One day she found out this woman had a sister who was in a lot of trouble and had an illegitimate child she was trying to palm off on anybody that would take it. Miss Laura was outraged by this and she convinced her secretary to take the child and raise it up with her own baby, which was due to arrive any day. That was how Alex come to the house.

"Now this secretary she didn't care much for the baby. Alex was two when she come to us, I was five. She said Alex got in the way a lot, so she wound up leaving her in the kitchen with my mother and I all day. She fixed this room up for her down there so she didn't have to spend no time with the family at all. Then, when Diana was born, Miss Laura was so took with her she seemed to forget all about Alex and only asked about her when she spoke to my mother about the menu.

"Alex knew all this but it didn't matter to her. My mother loved her more than any mother could love her own child. Sometimes I thought she loved Alex more than me but she always told me that Alex was unwanted and didn't belong nowhere whereas I was my mother's own blood as anyone could see. Alex was a good child, too, and she returned my mother's love. She called her 'Mama' until the day she died and on that day she closed herself up in the kitchen and wouldn't come out, even for Diana."

"How did you feel about that?" I asked.

"Her grief was real," she said simply. "I understood Alex, I always have. When she was little she was like my sister. We went to the same school, the public school. Diana went to a private school and for a long time she didn't associate with Alex and me much. She was a willful, mean child and gave her mother nothing but grief. She amused herself by treating Alex like an idiot because she couldn't read very well. She used to come drag Alex out of the kitchen and take her upstairs to drill her on her lessons and laugh at her until she was in tears. That made her reading worse, of course, but it wasn't really from lack of trying. She just always did have that trouble. I think it was because she was treated badly before she come to us. My mother tried to teach her, I did too, but her teachers at school didn't seem to care much.

There was one that found out she can memorize anything, even long poems, if she just hears them a few times, and he also found out she can do figuring in her head. Did you know that?"

"No," I said.

"She can add a line of numbers in her head faster than you could with one of those machines. Anyhow, Diana found out about this, too, and gradually she began to treat Alex a little more respectfully. As she got older she got real interested in Alex, partly, I guess, 'cause Alex was turning out so pretty and had a kind of sultry way about her that made Diana's beaux turn around when she come in the room. Alex was proud too, my mother had made her that way, and she wouldn't be treated like a servant. The two of them had been watching each other all their lives and it was natural, my mother said, that they would finally come together. Diana started coming to Alex's room after her dates, to tell her what happened I guess, and pretty soon she was down there half the time.

"They was both popular girls, both of them being so pretty, but naturally Diana got a better class of boy than Alex. She got it in her head that Alex was throwing herself away on mean low boys, which she was, as a matter of fact, and she started bringing Alex out on her dates with her and taking her to the country club. Alex always went along like a dog but it was for Diana she went, not for any of those rich boys. She had spent too long in the kitchen to care about money. She's like that to this day. That's what Diana don't understand about her."

"What were you doing all this time?" I asked.

"Well, I was older than them and I looked out for them as much as I could. It was hurting my mother to see Alex coming in at four in the morning in Diana's silk dresses with society boys breathing down her neck. It was like she lost her baby. Then, when they was both still in high school, I got pregnant and had a son, so I was occupied."

"Where is he now?" I asked.

"My boy? He's in school in the North. He goes to a private school. Diana believes he's an artist and I guess she may be right." She said this quickly, with a defiant pride, as if it explained why she was wasting her time talking to me.

"How old is he?"

"He's fifteen."

I was silent, hoping she would return to her story. The vision I had of Alex in borrowed finery, sniffing indifferently at the advances of the rich, filled me with excitement.

"The thing was," she picked up her story, "neither of them girls was too interested in men, they thought they was above all that. If Diana found a man she liked, she thought she should pass him on to Alex, and Alex was the same way. The poor boys was so confused they didn't know which way was up. Sometimes they made the mistake of treating Alex like a servant and when that happened Diana would cut them dead. She threw a cut-glass vase at one who told her she shouldn't hang around with Alex 'cause everyone knew she was nothing but a penniless slut. Diana thought Alex was something rare, and exotic, like one of them little cats people bring up from South America that are always wild and tear up the house.

"Alex was wild, too. She took up wild things. She took up that knife throwing, mostly 'cause Diana thought it was a fine thing to do. She rides a horse better than Diana and she knows how to care for them. She learned how to fix cars. She took up singing because Diana liked to have her sing Italian songs while she was working on her car. She had complete freedom in the house, and when they both went to college, Diana convinced her mother that Alex should move upstairs in the room next to her own. Her mother didn't like it much but she was never in the habit of denying Diana a thing.

"When they was in college they had the only trouble I ever known them to have over a man. He was a worthless creature Alex picked up in a bar somewhere. He bragged and swaggered and he had no education but he was a fine man to look at and he made Alex laugh. He came around the house a few times and when he saw Diana and learned where the money really was he started trying to play them against each other. How he got as far as he did I'll never understand but someway he come between them. I think Alex had taken a strong fancy to him and didn't want to give him up. Diana was attracted to him because he was such a smart little hustler, she thought he had courage, but it was just cheap nerve. One night he come to the house and there was a devil of a fight and the end of it was he left with Diana and she said she wasn't coming back.

"Her mother was fit to die. She pulled her hair right out of her head and went crying to Alex's room and said what should she do and where was Diana and how could they save her beautiful child. Alex treated her cold. She just went downstairs and took the keys to one of the big cars and drove off. Miss Laura was in such a state they had to call a doctor and then she got the doctor to call the police. But about the time the police arrived and started asking questions, Alex drove up with Diana in the car. I was standing on the porch and I remember Diana had her head in her hands and Alex drove up real fast and slammed on the brakes hard so that Diana fell forward. She just let herself fall and Alex got out, went around the car, and pulled her out by the arm. Then I saw Diana was crying. That was the only time I ever seen her cry. They come up to the house and Alex's face was white and her mouth was grim, she was a sight. She sort of pushed Diana at me when they come up and then she went inside and strode past Miss Laura, who was trying to get ahold of her so she could kiss her. She brushed her off and went up to her room, slamming the door behind her. I was trying to comfort poor Diana, she was crying like she was going to die. Finally she got herself calmed down and she went inside and drank two glasses of brandy real fast. Her mother was carrying on but she paid her no mind. Then she went up to Alex's door and beat on it with her fist but Alex wouldn't answer. She said, 'I'm going to stay by this door until you let me in.'

"And she did. She got her pillow and lay down in front of that door and refused to go to bed. Her mother was so worn out she gave up arguing and went to her own bed. In the morning I went up and Diana wasn't there. The two of them came down to breakfast together and they didn't say a word about it, but seemed real pleased with each other."

She paused and gave me a long quizzical look. "And that brings us round to your question," she said.

"What do you mean?"

"Who it is you look like." She raised her eyebrows as if to allow me the obvious conclusion, but I was so taken with this new image of Alex I failed to see it.

"You look like him," she said. "That man they had the fight over."

I felt a strange tingling in my spine, as if someone had touched me.

"Of course, you're older," she continued. "And you're lighter built. But otherwise, the resemblance . . ."

There was the sound of a door closing, then rapid soft footsteps on the stairs. Collie got up abruptly and turned to the sink, finishing her sentence under her breath. "When I saw you coming up that walk it gave me a chill." She looked up at the doorway and I followed her gaze. Diana stood smiling in the frame.

"Good morning," she said cheerfully. She was dressed in a loose white blouse that came down to her hips. My first impression was that she wore nothing else and then I found myself staring pointedly at the legs of her white linen shorts. Her long pale legs ended in sandals, also white. This costume, combined with her ungainly figure, gave her an air of jaunty good humor. She came into the kitchen and dropped into a chair, crossing her legs neatly beneath the curve of her stomach.

"You want eggs?" Collie asked her.

"No," she said. "Just coffee."

Collie set a cup before her and pushed the plate of rolls toward her. "Eat something," she said. "That child will be born with the jitters."

"I'll wait until Alex gets up." She helped herself to two rolls as she said this. Then, balancing them on the rim of her saucer, she got up and left the room. A few moments later I heard the first bright measures of a Bach Invention.

I sat at the table looking at my hands. My head was buzzing with ideas. I wanted to talk to Diana alone, before Alex got up, though I didn't know what I wanted her to say to me.

"Go on," Collie said, startling me. "She's waiting for you."

I pushed my cup away. "I know," I said.

I passed down the hall and stopped near the door of Diana's music room. She had finished the Invention and was playing the languorous piece she had played the night before. I stood in the doorway watching her back, which did not look like that of a pregnant woman. She finished and said, without turning, "Come in."

I went in, feeling unaccountably shy but eager for a conversation with her. "You play beautifully," I said.

She turned a little, still keeping her face averted from me as if she didn't wish me to see it. She indicated a chair just behind her. "Sit down," she said.

I took my chair and watched her as she flipped through the pages of a music book. "What was that you just played?"

"Brahms," she said. "An intermezzo."

"You played it last night," I said. "As I was falling asleep, I listened to it."

She selected a page and set the book on the piano's music rack. "Did you sleep well?" she asked, turning to me at last.

"I did sleep well," I said. I looked into her eyes, which were pale and flecked with bits of silver. She glanced up, over my head, and the pupils contracted a little, then she looked back at me. I had the feeling she was trying to make me look up, though why she would have done so I couldn't tell. I thought that she was a little insane and I felt myself tensing, preparing for something absurd, something shocking.

"Did you dream?" she asked.

"No," I said. "I slept too deeply. When I woke up I thought I had just fallen asleep."

She rubbed her eyes quickly and looked at me again, as if she were having difficulty focusing on me. "I envy you," she said. "I don't sleep at all any more."

"Because of the baby?" I asked.

Her hands strayed to her great belly and she smiled to herself. "Would you like to touch him?" she said.

My impulse was to draw away but I held my hand out steadfastly and she leaned toward me, taking my hand and guiding it over the silky material of her long blouse. The skin beneath it was remarkably hard, it didn't feel like skin at all but like some tough animal hide. Her hand stopped, pressing down on my own, and then beneath my fingers there was a sure hard kick, so abrupt and so strong that I felt momentarily a tiny heel rippling from my fingers to my palm. I pulled my hand away, startled. "Does it hurt?" I asked.

She smiled. "Not at all. It's reassuring. He's so strong."

"He is," I agreed. "Don't you feel invaded?"

She laughed. "Invaded?" she said. "Yes, I suppose I do. It makes me rebellious."

"Yet you seem calm," I lied.

She scowled, turning back to the piano. "I know how I seem," she said. "Would you like me to play for you?"

"I would," I said. My chair was comfortable and the music she had chosen was brilliantly simple, a Mozart sonata. Her hands moved expertly across the keys, the wrist turning slightly out on staccato notes. She played a sequence of chords, leaning forward and raising her shoulders a little, then her back relaxed as she played a passage of ascending

arpeggios. The music was bright and as she came to its conclusion the sun, escaping clouds outside, sent light streaming
through the window. My spirits lifted.

She finished, leaning into the last chord, then turned to me.
"Do you like music?" she asked.

"I do," I said, "very much. My mother played the violin."

"Do you play any instruments?"

"I don't. Unfortunately."

She nodded. "It is unfortunate. I always hope my guests
will play some instrument, but that's rarely the case. I don't
know of any pleasure greater than making music with another person."

"I can imagine," I said.

"No you can't," she replied pleasantly. "Not ever having
done it. It is a pure intellectual pleasure, better than the best
conversation and at the same time a deep sensual pleasure,
more stimulating and more intimate than sex."

"I see," I said. "I can't imagine it."

She smiled. "It doesn't matter," she said. "It may well be
my own fantasy. Sharing music is the best camaraderie I've
had."

"You must be lonely, then," I said. "Playing here alone.
Like talking to yourself."

She looked surprised, but pleasantly so. "Yes," she said.
"It is just like that. I suppose that's why I feel uncomfortable
when someone listens." She gave me a cool curious look that
pleased me. I liked her frankness and her lack of flirtatious-
ness but I found myself unable to determine how she was
reacting to me. Did I please her, or was she bored?

She interrupted my thoughts. "How do you come to be
with Alex?" she asked flatly.

"By good luck," I said.

"You don't find her overbearing?"

"No. Why should I?"

"No reason," she said, turning her attention to her music
book. "Many people do, though."

"Do you?"

Her eyebrows lifted and she pursed her lips, controlling a smile. "Don't be foolish," she said.

"Who does, then?" I insisted.

"People who don't know her as we do, obviously," she said. "Do you mind if I change the subject abruptly?"

"Not at all."

"I want to tell you this while I'm thinking of it." She pushed her book away from her and folded her hands over her stomach as if she were prepared to give a recitation. "There is a man on the grounds here whom you may see."

"Banjo," I said.

She looked alarmed. "How did you know his name?"

"Alex showed me the letter you wrote her asking her to come here," I said. "You mentioned that he was here."

"She showed you that letter?"

"Yes," I said.

"And you remember his name. How remarkable."

"I have a good memory," I said.

"Yes. Well. I see that." She paused.

"What about Banjo?"

She regained her composure. "He is a drunken man of no use to anyone. He's allowed to stay on here as a gardener, but it's only through the largesse of my family, as he doesn't know a weed from a flower and would be too lazy to do anything about it if he did."

"I see," I said.

"I would consider it a personal favor if, should you run into him, you would not speak with him."

"Would he want to speak to me?"

"He will speak to anyone who will listen and many who would rather not. And many who should not."

"What will he tell me?"

"Lies," she said. "May I extract this promise from you?" She gave me a look of courteous interest, but I felt behind it the implacability of her will.

94

"If you want it," I said, "then you have it."

She smiled. "I think you are a remarkable man," she said.

"In what way?" I said.

"You have made me like you and I was prepared not to."

"Then I'm satisfied," I said.

She turned to her piano and began playing an amusing fanfare, as if to signal the completion of an alliance between us. I listened for a few moments. Then, hearing voices in the kitchen, I got up and went out to find Alex, upon whom, I thought, everyone in the house was waiting.

In the hall I had an alarming thought. Suppose Diana's music was a prearranged signal to the two women in the kitchen. When I reached my destination I found Alex cracking eggs into a bowl while Collie, at her side, stirred a pot of bubbling grits. Collie was smiling over her task, amused by something Alex had said. Alex's expression was more restrained but she was clearly in a good humor. She held her hand out to me and brushed my mouth with her fingertips as I passed by. "Are you hungry?" she said.

"No. I ate these rolls."

Collie turned from her cooking to ring the crystal bell over her stove. A moment later Diana's music stopped and she joined us. "So, Alex," she said. "You still sleep late."

Alex mumbled. Her good mood had evaporated and she was tense. I glanced from her to Diana, who stood large and beautiful in the doorway, her hands raised on either side, pressing against the jambs, her wide strange eyes bright and full of good will. "Shall we have breakfast?" she continued.

Alex attacked her bowl of eggs with a fork. "That's just what we're fixing to do," she said.

I felt ill at ease. The women needed a private conversation and I was an intruder. Diana began setting places at the table, her arm brushing my own as she passed.

"I thought I'd go for a walk," I said to the air.

"Aren't you going to eat?" Diana asked.

"No," I said. "I don't have much appetite in the morning. I'll just have another cup of coffee and then I'll go."

"Where will you go?" Alex asked without turning from her work.

"In the woods, I thought," I said.

"You'd better take a compass," Collie suggested. She set her bowl on the table, and opening the drawer beneath, she withdrew a shiny silver compass, which she held out to me. I took it and stood looking down at the trembling needle.

"It's easy to become confused on the grounds," Diana said, "but as long as you're on Beaufort's land there are plenty of clear paths. That's the only work I can get out of Banjo. For some reason it interests him."

"It's his labyrinth," Alex said, "in which he hopes to snare us all."

"Yes, well," Diana agreed, "we are smarter than he."

"That's not an accomplishment," Alex replied. She turned from the stove, pushing the now cooked eggs from the pan onto a plate. As she did this her eyes met Diana's and she smiled apologetically. I couldn't see Diana's face, but when she turned to me and offered to walk with me to the edge of the wood, her features were composed.

"No," I said. "Eat your breakfast. I'm sure I can find my way." I left the three women drawing their chairs up to the table and went down the hall and out across the lawn.

8

The lawn was wide and green, rolling down from the house and ending abruptly in a stand of pine trees. The air was still. I was content as I walked, finding pleasure in details, such as the fact that the shoes Alex had bought me were comfortable and I was neither hungry nor thirsty and the smell in the air was sweet, damp, a mixture of pine and jasmine. A sweet-olive tree spread its gray branches between me and the woods and the smell of its bark as I passed intoxicated me. Before going in among the trees I stopped to look up at the sky, vast and speckled with clouds like schools of small fish. The sun was already high overhead. There it whirled, or there I whirled beneath it, and it was blindingly serene, bathing the air and the earth in light. I asked myself why I didn't look up more often.

I thought, as I stepped into the shade of the trees, that I had been bogged down in something thick, foul, evil for as long as I could remember but that now I was free. I had kicked my way clear without even knowing. Mine had always been the heartless struggle of an animal who has the intelligence to comprehend the efficient calculation of the trap into which he has stumbled. Somehow, in spite of my hopelessness, I had escaped it. Now, I thought, I would walk in the woods every day, I would run. The women would carry on without me, and when they needed me, Diana would send one of her dogs out to find me.

I strode through the trees. For a while my way was clear, the ground was strewn with pine needles, and there was little vegetation. Gradually the pine trees thinned out, replaced by cypress and oak. Grasses and vines appeared on the path and a hard woody fungus clung to the exposed roots of the trees. There were a few low bushes and some thorny branches blocked the way, catching on my pants legs so that I had to stop to pull them loose. As the foliage grew thicker I discerned a path, worn by feet and cleared by a blade. I began, without thinking, to follow it. Soon I had no choice, for the path was hemmed in by a tropical forest, thick, sinewy, dark, and buzzing with life. I took out my compass and determined that I was heading north. Overhead I could still see the sky but only in leafy patches. The air was cool and the leaves that brushed against me were still damp with dew.

I thought of Diana and of my brief interview with her. She was in every way a superior woman. Her size, her beauty, her musical ability, her candor, her intelligence, all these qualities rose to my mind as evidence for my conclusion, but nothing, save a willing admiration, rose with it. I did not want her. When I sat between her and Alex at the table, when I saw them together, I wanted to be unseen, so that I might watch them and not influence them. At the same time I wanted to take Alex away with me. It was Alex and only Alex I wanted. In spite of her murderous temper, her secretiveness, her semi-literacy, her insatiability (which she hid whenever she could, being, for some reason, ashamed of it), it was she whom I desired.

But Diana interested me. The prospect of further conversations with her intrigued me. I did not know what she was to Alex but there was some tie between them I felt I must ferret out. I wanted to know, and feared to know, the full and exact extent of it. My own resemblance to the man who had caused them a serious quarrel would make this more difficult but I didn't imagine it to be a serious impediment. Surely neither Diana nor Alex would be so naïve as to set much store in such an accident. I had no wish to cause either of them any unhappiness and I thought they knew this.

My path forked ahead of me and I chose the left branch. A look at my compass confirmed my suspicion that I was traveling in a large circle. A few yards farther on, the path forked again and again I chose the left branch, thinking that in this way I wouldn't become confused when I decided to go back. When I stood still I could hear the motion of insects on the ground and birds in the trees. I felt as though I were on some unexplored planet and I realized that, except for a few weekend excursions with friends, I had never walked in such a place before. I had always lived in the city, had always been one wall away from the next person's life. My defense had been to live alone in my rooms. Here, I thought, I had the freedom I had always suspected could be possible— pleasant society, perfect solitude, whatever I wished.

I thought of Alex, as Collie had described her to me, and as I had seen her the night before. I recalled how she looked another time, that last night we spent in my empty apartment. She sat up amid the swirl of sheets and absently trimmed her toenails with a pair of scissors she had found in my pathetic box of possessions. She kept her back straight and propped her foot high up on her knee, her face turned slightly away from me. She was languorous and abstracted and I wanted to ask her what she was thinking, but certain that she would give me her veiled look, her cool "nothing," I contented myself in watching her performance. As I inspected this image a thought occurred to me, clear and unmistakable. I had never reached her, never touched her, she was unmoved and unmarked by me.

As she was, I added, by all men. I stumbled on my path and felt a thorough confusion in my thinking, a general search and alarm. Was it true? And if so, did it matter?

When I regained my balance, I gave myself this answer. It was true that she didn't have much feeling for me and there was a sense in which this fact didn't matter. Had I really any feeling for her, save obsessive lust? But there was also the possibility that she (or I) might be changed, that I might find a way to push past her self-possession and make myself known. As I envisioned her, turning her relentless attention from one foot to the other, I knew what that way was.

For Alex and for me, there was one dazzling truth, that there is, in this life, no separation of the mind from the body. One may be at war with the other, but it is at best a corrupt war in which both sides are so saturated with spies and counter-spies that it is no longer possible to determine who works for whom. The spies themselves do not know. The struggle is aimless, futile, and will only end when a third force, dark and powerful, comes from without and levels everything, the armies, the spies, the field of battle.

Could one person provide this force for another, could love (or lust or whatever it was—passion, obsession) be the leveler? I thought that if I could force Alex's body to acknowledge me, then her mind must follow, or vice versa. I chose to attempt a sensual possession, as I would not have known (and still do not know) where to begin to engage her thinking. Besides, I suspected that in Alex the battle between the senses and the spirit was, at the moment, uneven; that her sensuality had the upper hand.

I thought of her pleasure and determined that it should be first in all my considerations. I wanted only to make her pleasure my own, and in spite of the unexpected results of my plan (which I maintain I never desired), I wanted nothing more.

How would I do this? I felt that I knew when I pleased her; she was not one of those obstinate women who refuse to admit they have been pleased. I would seek out those instances and amplify them. If I could make her sigh (and I could), then I could do more.

I would have to get through to her at that moment when she held out on me so perversely, in our lovemaking. It was always there, her reservation, her impenetrability, her amusement at my own great rapture, a restraint that, I thought, she took for pleasure, though it was not she who was most gratified.

There were things I could do. My past experience with women suggested a few. I had, I reflected, never had a woman I thought worth the effort I knew I could make. The idea delighted me so that I wanted to dash back to the house and carry Alex off upstairs with me at once. I imagined her profile and anticipated how it would look when her breathlessness was deep and frightening to her. I wanted to shake her and say, "Do you think I don't know how you've been faking it?" I controlled myself with an effort. I flexed my hands, which were strong in spite of the pain they caused me and which, I thought, I would use most skillfully to bring Alex to such transports that she would deny me nothing.

It seemed a good, clear, workable idea, one of the few I've had in my life, and as I considered how I would undertake it I thought myself particularly lucid. It did not occur to me that I would fail, or rather that I would succeed in ways I had not anticipated; that I would be sorry and sick and dead wrong.

I hurried on along my path as if I expected to find Alex herself at the end of it. The sun was bright and hot and I realized that I was too warm, that my shirt was clinging to my back and my throat was parched. My path was narrow and obstructed by small bushes and vines, the forest threatened to wipe it out entirely. I was on the verge of turning back when it widened and at the next curve I found myself in a shady clearing where the grass was manicured and beds of carefully tended marigolds lined a walk that led to a bower of sweet peas and roses. Inside that bower was a wooden lawn chair and next to it a small table. The scene was so inviting and so completely unexpected that I paused for a moment before stepping into it. A gnarled and sprawling oak provided shade for the place and as I admired its girth I noticed something glinting in a hollow of the trunk. Closer inspection revealed, set down in the hollow, a blue ceramic jug. My head was ringing so from the heat that I thought this discovery appropriate. I withdrew my treasure and took it to the table, where I uncorked it carefully. The scent that rose through the hot sticky air was unmistakably bourbon. I lifted the jug to my dry lips and drank deeply. It was very good bourbon and no sooner had I drunk it than I sat down upon the chair in a wonderful stupor.

I sat for a long time. I may have fallen asleep. The air was cool when I came to myself, my skin was cool and dry. I looked up into the sweet-flowered bower and thought I would never leave Beaufort unless I was forced to go. I corked the bottle up and returned it to its niche in the tree, wishing for a piece of paper and a pen so that I might thank my benefactor. I stood looking out at the bower and past it to the edge of the forest, a circle of impenetrable jungle, full, no doubt, of snakes and exotic insects. I thought I knew who was responsible for the place. Indeed, Diana had said that Banjo tended the paths of her property. I wondered if she knew of this spot. Alex, I recalled, had said that Banjo's maze was a trap. I decided that, as I had come to this place by consistently choosing the path to the left, on my next visit I would try the other route, continually taking the right. Would I meet the architect of the labyrinth? I did not doubt that I would. And would I speak to him in spite of my promise to Diana? I thought, considering the advantage I had taken of his hospitality, that I must. As I mused over this I had the cold and certain sensation that I was being watched. Again I scanned the edge of the jungle. Halfway round the circle my heart contracted and my hand clenched into a ball in my pocket. There, crouched just beyond the outer layer of foliage, was the shadowy outline of a man, though all I could really see of him was one hand. It was a strangely cramped and simian hand, as black as if it had been charred in a fire. As I watched, it was withdrawn from my view. I turned abruptly and set off down the path, not running but walking briskly, so that sometime later, when I arrived on the lawn of Beaufort, I was sweating again and out of breath.

As I came out across the lawn I heard someone singing, a woman's voice, clear and high, coming from the house. I recognized it as Alex's, though it had little in common with her speaking voice, which, I realized, was somewhat harsh and tense. This was rhapsodic singing. The piano accompaniment was dramatic, repeated chords that vibrated beneath the melody line, building in intensity as the voice sought higher notes, greater contrasts. I hurried toward it.

I found them in the music room, Diana at the piano, Alex standing behind her, addressing her song to the window, Collie deep in the chair I had occupied during my earlier interview. They didn't notice me.

My heart was lifted by the sight of them, all lost in the music, intent, transported by their friendship, their beauty, and their power. They were not ordinary women.

No, I thought then, they are mad and cruel and wear their freedom like a mantle, rendering them invisible to lesser creatures, but that thought, whimsical and shocking, left me with only an unarticulated sense of admiration.

Alex came to the end of her song. "*Mentre nel suo segreto il cor piagato s'angoscia e si martora.*" As she did she turned and looked at me. Diana finished a measure after her, held the final chord so that its resonance filled and completed the fluctuations of the air waves. Then she, too, turned to me.

"What a dramatic little song," Alex said.

"What's it about?" I asked.

Diana turned back to her music, flipping through the pages in search of something else. "Actually," she said, "it's very charming. The whole thing is just an elaborate metaphor in which the sun's light on calm water is compared to the smiles on many faces." She paused, having found what she was looking for, and flattened the pages with her palm. Then she turned on the bench to look at me. "Both," she concluded, "hide tempestuous depths."

"Like Alex's smile," I said, for she was gazing at me with a look of deceptive calm.

Diana laughed. "Exactly," she said. "How was your walk?"

What she wanted to know was whether I had seen Banjo or not. What I wanted was to get Alex upstairs with me so that I could begin my premeditated seduction. I would start with something simple, like brushing her hair. "Long," I said, "and tiring. Do I have time for a bath before lunch?"

Collie, who had been sitting quietly in her chair, watching us lazily like a woman watching children, said, "Yes. You have forty-five minutes."

"I won't be that long," I said, turning to leave. I caught Alex's eye as I did and I raised my brows in what I hoped was a friendly and suggestive expression. She smiled; my antics amused her. I went upstairs, hoping that she would follow.

The bath was a large one, big enough for two. I turned on the faucets and watched the rush of water splattering on the porcelain. I could hear Alex singing downstairs, a more sprightly song than the last. I liked the way her voice paused before attempting high notes, then hit them full and sure, as if she had shot an arrow and hit the exact center of her target. I undressed and got into the tub, recoiling momentarily, for the water was very hot, then sinking down until the water came to my chin. The song ended and there was quiet. I decided to put my head underwater so that I could listen to the vibrations in the floors and walls. I closed my eyes and sank down, holding my breath as water rushed into my ears and nose. I was thinking that sound came to me in the same way it must come to Diana's baby, in liquid waves. When I opened my eyes Alex was standing over me, looking down through the water with an expression of concern. I surfaced.

"I knocked," she said, "but you didn't answer. I thought you might be dead."

"Excuse me," I said, mopping my face with the cloth.

"Do you always do that?"

"No," I said. "Not always."

"You look like a lobster."

"The water is very warm."

She sat on the edge of the tub and dabbled her hand in the water. "How can you take such a hot bath on such a hot day?"

"It refreshes me," I said.

"It's like some sort of purge," she said.

I sat up and rubbed my hair with the cloth.

"Would you rather be alone?" she asked.

"I'd rather you got in here with me."

She smiled, wide-eyed. "I don't think we have time."

"Just put your feet in, then," I suggested. "Pull that chair up and I'll wash your feet for you. Just like in the Bible. It'll relax you."

She reached for the chair. "You're crazy," she said. She was wearing cloth shoes, which she kicked off easily, presenting me with her long pale feet. I soaped up my cloth.

"What did you find on your walk?" she said. "You were gone a long time."

"I found a comfortable chair and a bottle of bourbon."

She leaned back a little in her chair so that her feet went to the ankles in water. I massaged the arches with my thumbs. "That feels marvelous," she said.

It felt marvelous to me, too, though I didn't tell her. If she had looked at the water's surface she would have seen, rising there, stiff evidence of how pleasant I found my occupation. But her head was back on the chair and she gazed at the ceiling. I took her left big toe into my mouth and sucked it gently.

"That feels odd," she said, but she didn't pull away. She was talkative. "I was glad you went off because it gave me a chance to find out what Diana thinks of you."

I moved to the next toe.

"She said she thought you were agreeable."

I lifted my lips from my teeth and said, around the toe I retained, "I am."

"I know it." She laughed. Then, seriously, "Do you like it here?"

I moved to the next toe.

"Does that mean yes?"

I repeated the action.

"I suppose this is how language began," she mused.

I continued this dalliance for a few minutes longer, until I felt she was relaxed. I could see about her mouth and in the way her hands moved along the side of her chair that she experienced some little tension still, the tension of expectation. I washed her feet carefully and dried them with a towel, then I lay back in the water.

Her eyes opened, then she sat up. "Are you stopping?" she asked.

I wrung out the cloth and held it out before me. "If you don't mind," I said, "I think I'd like to lie very still in this water for a while."

"You want to be alone?" She asked this as if the idea was a novel and pleasant one.

"If you don't mind?"

"Of course not," she protested. She took her sandals and stood up, looking down at me. "I'll see you downstairs," she said.

"I won't be long," I replied as she went out. I spread the cloth over my face and closed my eyes, so pleased with myself that I smiled at my own invention.

9

At dinner that night Alex treated me with bemused curiosity, as if she thought I might reveal something interesting, some grain of truth or something paradoxical and multi-faceted. Later, when she came to my room, she stood in the doorway looking in, alert and anxious. I was writing at the desk. I put my pen down and said, "Come in."

She didn't move. "Diana wanted me to sing," she said, "but I was irresistibly drawn to your door."

"You say that as if you think you've made the wrong choice."

"I've no way of knowing," she said. She came in and sat on the edge of my bed.

I went to her and sat beside her. She slipped her arm around my back and rested her head in my lap. I stroked the smooth skin of her neck and shoulders, wondering at the dry sensation in my throat. My impulse was to throw her back across the bed and plunge into her, deeply and thoroughly, but I controlled myself, determined not to make a move until she gave some evidence of desiring it. After a while she turned so that my hand fell across her breasts. Her head slipped off my knee and she lay gazing at the ceiling above her.

She appeared to be relaxed but I could feel her tension and I knew she was drawing herself away so that she could receive me absently, dreamily, through a haze.

It took a long time, nearly two hours. I spent most of that time on a tightrope of desire, moving with caution but surely, steadily. My destination swayed and rippled before me like a mirage. I watched her face as she moved beneath me, her eyes closed, her mouth slightly ajar, and I felt her attempts to elude me. When she seemed to wait for me, I slowed down; when she pressed her palms into my back I went faster, pulling her hips up off the bed with me. Her back was very flexible and she seemed to want to have it bent, farther and farther. At one point she caught her ankles in her hands, pulling her legs back until I thought her spine must snap. Gradually I began to have some success. Her sighs were long and came from deep within. Her eyes rolled back beneath the lids and she bit her lower lip hard so that when she released it a mark remained. Suddenly her eyes flew open and she looked at me, breathless and surprised. "What are you doing to me?" she said. I was unable to speak so I smiled and drew her up to kiss her. Her mouth opened beneath mine and she thrust her tongue out greedily.

When we were done she lay face down on the pillow, her arms and legs spread wide. I lay on my back beside her, feeling spent but still excited. After a few moments she moaned, a theatrical moan that expressed pleasure as well as exhaustion. When she turned her face to me her eyes were damp and she smiled self-consciously. "God damn, Claude," she said. "What happened?"

Good, good, I thought, I was right. I pulled her to me and spread her hair out across my chest and arms. She nuzzled her head against my side, pressing her lips to my skin softly, repeatedly, absentmindedly, until she fell asleep.

The next morning after breakfast she asked me if I was still interested in seeing her throw her knives. I was indeed, I said, and followed her across the yard, carrying her case for her and smiling at the way she pulled her hair up and pinned it in preparation for the serious business ahead. She showed me the target, which stood under some trees near the edge of the woods, and, taking the case from me, suggested that I try a throw myself.

"I don't think so," I said.

"Come on," she said. "It's not hard, really." She opened the case and held it out before me and I gazed at the blades gleaming in the morning sun.

"All right," I said. "I'll try one. Where do I stand?"

She led me to a spot about twenty feet from the target. I chose my knife.

"Hold it like this," she said, taking my hand. "And throw it by flicking your wrist out so that it'll turn over in the air."

I did as she instructed. The knife sailed through the air and for a moment I thought I had done well, but it fell to the ground about a foot short of the target.

Alex laughed. "Try another."

I took a second knife and this time I was more careful. It hit the outer ring of the target and hung there for a few seconds before falling out.

"Good," Alex said. "Most people can't do that well."

"I want to see you do it," I said.

She went to the target and picked up the two knives. "The hard thing is," she said when she returned, "to throw them one after another at an even interval."

"How long?"

"Well, I've done it at three seconds but not very well. I'll do it at five." She took the three remaining knives from the case and handed them to me. I found them awkward to hold but she showed me how to lay them across my palms so that the handles faced her. "Should I count?" I said.

"No," she said, "I can feel the time." She turned to face the target and stood for a moment with her hands at her sides, her head dropped forward a little. Then suddenly I felt the first knife, followed by the other four, being drawn from my hands.

She threw five knives five seconds apart, so quickly that I didn't really see it happen. When she was through they hung upon the red circle at the center of the target like quivers thrust into a bull. I turned to her. She stood gazing at the target, shielding her eyes with one hand, the other hanging loosely at her side. "That's what you do to me," she said, looking at me.

I laughed.

"Perfect aim," she said, walking away toward the target. "Perfect timing."

And that was how I knew I had succeeded in making myself indispensable to her.

For some time things went along well; the surface of our lives was remarkably calm. My own life was changed; the character of it was changed and I was elevated by it and felt myself to be better and stronger than I had been. I fell into agreeable routines. I walked in the woods every day and was soon familiar with the paths, all of which led, I concluded, to the same tree I had discovered on my first walk, or to dead ends. Most mornings I went out early, before it was too warm, and I often found Diana up and about, in the house or on the lawn. She prowled, she said, in search of sleep. Once she walked with me awhile and entertained herself by naming the plants we encountered. Usually I was alone. I sat in the clearing; sometimes I walked aimlessly, sometimes I ran. I found the latter peculiarly exhilarating; I made it my goal to run quickly and as quietly as possible. I became so expert at it that occasionally I surprised a porcupine or a raccoon.

I returned from the woods in time to bathe before lunch. After this meal, which was a light one, Alex joined me and we passed the afternoon in each other's company. Diana slept during this time, or so she said, for we often heard her pacing up and down in her room. Collie retired to her own room. Sometimes Alex and I went out on the porch, or smoked cigarettes in the library, or walked together, but most often we found our way to my room, where I continued my invasion of her senses. She was willing to have me do so.

I had made a crucial discovery about her. Her sensuality was so near the surface of her consciousness that it was a functional part of her personality, and once aroused, she could no more turn it off than she could stop her eyes, once opened, from seeing or her ears from hearing. It was unlike anything I had ever seen before, like finding a mate from a different, unexpected world. All comparison was idle, but once I found myself thinking of Mona thrashing about, working like a laborer to arrive at her deliberate pleasure; it was something she pursued and pounced upon. And I recalled how she had left me cold, so distant and indifferent that I couldn't look at her and had to endure her infantile effusions with my face turned away. For Alex, I thought, pleasure was surprise. She still tried to elude me; that, I thought, was an automatic defense. But as we spent more time together she began to trust me, even, I thought, to turn herself over to me with a willingness that touched me. I wanted nothing more than to witness again and again the spectacle of her surrender.

One evening, as we sat on the couch in my room and she, having insisted upon removing her boots without my assistance, leaned over her knees and pulled at the laces, I pressed my mouth against the nape of her neck and felt a shudder run the length of her spine. She turned to me and gave me an inquiring look so gentle and fearful that I thought she might suddenly jump up and run away if I spoke. I took her hands and kissed them, still watching her face. She closed her eyes and turned away. "Don't look at me," she said.

"But why?" I asked.

"I don't want to be seen," she said weakly. "I don't want to be known."

It was mild resistance, and I thought it wise at the time, based on the fear that the familiarity we shared, which was daily and complete, would spoil our mutual intoxication. I didn't give it much more thought than that.

In the evenings, after dinner, the four of us sat together in Diana's music room or on the porch. Diana could never be still long. Sometimes she paced before us, went to her piano, played awhile, then joined us again. Collie embroidered a large tablecloth and looked from one of us to the other, desultory and grave. I was never able to come any closer to her than I had that first morning. She spoke to me only when she had to, though there was nothing in her manner to suggest that she didn't wish to talk to me. On a few occasions, when we happened to be alone, I attempted to draw her out about Banjo. Why was he never mentioned, why did he never come to the house, how did she know he was there at all?

"He's there, all right," she said. "Biding his time."

"For what?" I said.

"For nothing," she replied. "Like most folks. Only he's such a fool, he don't know it."

A month passed in this way and I was content with everything. Then, on a particularly hot and humid night, I witnessed something I couldn't explain.

I awoke from a sound sleep to find my room flooded with moonlight; it was like day. Alex was not beside me, though she had been there when I fell asleep. I stretched and yawned and tried to go back to sleep but I felt agitated, my mind wandered. I knew I had been dreaming but couldn't recall the dream. I got up at last and went to the window. The moon was full and bright and the air was charged with light. I looked out across the lawn, toward the two sweet-olive trees. A movement beneath the trees caught my eyes and I was surprised to find myself looking at what could only be Diana's figure, stretched out on a blanket beneath the tree. As I watched, she sat up, turned to her side, then lay back down again. I wanted to open my window and call out to her but decided against it. It made me sad to think of her, sleepless, uncomfortable, wandering around in the night looking for a place to rest. I imagined her lying awake in her bed, pacing about her room, finally drawn by the moon and the still air, down the stairs and out on the lawn. She was wearing a white dressing gown and her hair, which she often pulled back, was loose, falling across her shoulders. As I watched she sat up again and looked toward the house. I stepped back from the window, not wishing to be seen. When I looked out again I saw someone else moving across the lawn. Diana stood while the smaller darker figure came close to her. Then she reached out her hand, drawing the other woman to her side and caressing the dark head.

It was Alex.

I closed my eyes and covered them with my hand. I had a sinking sensation. "Of course," I thought. When I opened my eyes again the blanket lay like a square of snow on the black grass. The women were gone.

Were they on the other side of the tree? Had they returned to the house?

I thought I saw a movement at the edge of the wood, then another close to the house, but I couldn't make it out. I turned away, feeling embarrassed; I felt I had been spying. My surprise at the sight of Alex was foolishness, I thought. She had walked out to see her friend; there was nothing remarkable in that. But something in the way she had moved, so quickly, so stealthily, bothered me, and when I reflected upon it, I was certain that Diana's gesture toward her had contained an element of tenderness I had never seen between them. I rubbed my head. The notion that their intimacy was deeper than I had suspected disturbed me, but I was not certain why. I felt a wave of nausea and sat down on the couch. The house was still around me and I listened for any sound, a footstep, a door closing, in vain. I put on my robe, opened my door, and went out into the hall. The quiet was intense. There was light under the door of Diana's room, but Alex's room was dark. I stood suspended, listening, for some time. Then I went down the hall and put my hand on the doorknob of Diana's door. It was cool and damp and I watched my hand with amazement as I turned the knob and pushed the door open before me.

I had never seen Diana's bedroom. Though I expected nothing extraordinary, I felt a rush of relief when I found myself looking into a pleasant tasteful room in which the only sign of disorder was the rumpled bed that had refused its owner any rest. Next to the bed was a small table on which stood a stack of books, night reading for the insomniac. I couldn't read the titles from where I stood. I hesitated, looked down the hall behind me, and stepped inside.

A book lay open across the bed. I glanced at the title, *Natural Childbirth*. It made me smile. Diana was determined to deliver her child as she wanted and her arguments with her doctor, whom she described as "intolerant and ignorant," made her tense with rage. She visited him weekly in the city and one of us always went with her. But she was independent and insisted upon running the boat herself, always on the flying bridge, where her thoughts were uninterrupted. When I accompanied her I didn't go to the doctor's with her but lay in the sun on the boat, drinking bourbon and reading.

I looked at the other books. Two were also about childbirth; another was a medical book. There was a biography of Mozart, a novel entitled *Dangerous Acquaintances*, and two books of music. Next to this was a small black leather-bound book with the word *Record* in gold letters across the font. I picked this one up and opened it. Page after page was filled with Diana's smooth curvilinear handwriting. I read this sentence, "The complexity of her character is a constant source of pleasure and surprise."

A sound at the door startled me and I snapped the book closed in my palm.

"This is most unexpected," Diana said. She stood in the doorway, her blanket draped across her arm, her hair streaming past her shoulders like a flood of light. I noticed that the top two buttons of her gown were open.

I felt like a child caught red-handed, and the absurd rush of my heartbeat, the weakness in my knees and stomach infuriated me. At the same time I was genuinely embarrassed. I set the book on the nightstand. "I didn't realize what it was," I said, "until I opened it. I read one sentence."

She took a step into the room. "And do you remember that sentence?"

I repeated what I had read.

"And to whom do you think I was referring?"

"I have no idea," I said. "It would be outrageous of me to speculate."

"You don't think investigating my room when I was absent a little outrageous?"

"Please, Diana," I said. "I apologize. I wasn't investigating. I wandered in here because I couldn't sleep."

"Did you think I would be able to help you?" She sat down in an armchair and draped her blanket across her lap. I couldn't gauge the degree of her disgruntlement.

"I saw you on the lawn," I said. "With Alex."

She raised her eyebrows. "I see," she said.

I stood looking at her, pleased with myself for managing to make my tawdry accusation so simply. I felt pleased with her, too. She was such a magnificent sight, her hands folded across her big stomach, her eyes darting about, glancing over my shoulder, at the rug near my feet, briefly at my own eyes, then settling on the empty air between us. "It's a remarkably hot night, don't you think?" she said. "If I could stand air-conditioning I would certainly try it." She wiped her upper lip with the side of her hand and smiled at me pleasantly.

"Perhaps something cool to drink," I suggested.

"Yes," she said. "I believe there's a bottle of champagne in the refrigerator downstairs."

"Shall I get it?"

"Yes, please," she said. "I feel very gay for some reason. Perhaps I should surprise an intruder more often."

"My heart was in my throat," I said.

"I saw that. It made blood rush to my head. I think it was a good experience for both of us."

I turned to go. "Don't bother with glasses," she said. "I have some here."

The moonlight poured in through every possible opening and I went to the kitchen without turning on any lights. I took the champagne from the refrigerator and stood in the icy glare of its light gazing at the label. It was expensive. I glanced past the bottle at my bare feet on the cold tiles. I felt awful. I realized that I had been thinking all the way down the stairs that I could not bear the hypocrisy that continually issued from my mouth. I didn't doubt that I received from others the same commodity I offered. The thought that Alex had gone out to Diana for whatever reasons had filled me with such pain and confusion that I had acted rashly, been caught in the act, and covered my rage with sarcasm, cleverness, and docility. I wanted to take the bottle upstairs and break it over Diana's lovely golden head. Instead, I opened it, aiming the cork at a light fixture and missing it entirely. I let the champagne bubble up over my hands and spill on the floor. Then I retraced my steps and brought the bottle to Diana's room.

She had passed her time in better spirits than I. She smiled and held out glasses to me amiably. I wondered about the man who looked like me. How could he have taken Diana away that night, how could any man, faced with the choice between Alex's irascible good sense and Diana's giddy but distant agreeableness—why would he have chosen Diana? She was like ice to me and her good humor only served to cool me down entirely. I drank my champagne and made polite conversation, excused myself, apologized again for snooping (was assured that my action had only offended her slightly), and went off to bed like a child reprimanded and reinstated in the graces of a benign mother. The whole thing irritated me.

More to the point was Alex's response the following morning. I had had a quiet breakfast with Collie, who interrupted my thoughts only twice, to inquire after my health and to request my assistance in the repair of a lawn mower. I was crossing the hall to go out for my walk when I heard a sound and turned to find Alex sitting on the steps smiling at me. She looked innocent and fresh, her hair pulled back and pinned at the nape of her neck. She had on jeans and a black pullover shirt, a stylized T-shirt with pleats at the shoulders. She sat with her legs stretched out on the stairs beneath her, her boots crossed at the ankles. Next to her lay her knife case and she rested one hand on it.

"You're up early," I said.

She jumped up, bringing the case with her, and came down to me.

"I know," she said. "I'll walk out with you."

"Don't you want breakfast?"

"I'll get it later." We crossed the porch and went out on the lawn. She was heading for her target and I followed her. She seemed very sure of herself, even cocky, and I amused myself by trying to get my hand under her shirt. She slapped at my fingertips and stepped out quickly ahead of me. "Watch out," she said. "I feel like I might kill this morning."

"Are you angry?" I asked.

She opened her case and removed one of the knives, brandishing it before me. "Just playful," she said. "I would kill accidentally, in play."

I caught her wrist and twisted her arm up behind her. I felt murderously playful myself. She winced but didn't drop the knife. I pressed my mouth against her neck. "Did you sleep well last night?" I said.

She ceased to struggle and I released her. "Sure," she said. "Why shouldn't I?"

"The moon was so bright."

She replaced the knife in its case. "Was it?" she said.

"Don't you remember?"

She didn't answer but stopped and turned to face me. I felt the air between us cool but I went on. "And you went out on the lawn."

She gave me a look of cold warning, I could not mistake it. Then she said, very slowly, as if to give me time to consider my plan, "Do you really have any idea what you're talking about?"

I thought it over. What, I wondered, was I trying to force her to say? What obligation was I trying to hold her to? "No," I said. "No, I don't."

She smiled. "Do you want to come and watch me practice?"

I felt peculiar. My head was swimming with suspicion. I looked past her at the edge of the woods.

"Go on, then," she said. "I'll see you later." She leaned toward me to give me a brief kiss, but I caught her by the shoulders and pulled her to me. I kissed her deeply and pressed her against me so abruptly that she lost her balance. I held her, one hand on the small of her back and my other arm wrapped tightly across her shoulders. She didn't resist. I felt the dread of losing her, the desire to possess her, and the certainty that each of these conditions would force me to endure the other. I released her and she stepped away from me.

I think I had a premonition then that I was about to lose her. Afterward, when I thought of that conversation, of that embrace, I saw it as a pinnacle, a meeting of equals. Our eyes met before we turned from one another and the look we exchanged was like what lions must share when they come upon one another in territory neither claims for its own. Pure surprise and admiration for one's own race, one's own kind.

We didn't speak. Alex went down to her target, her knife case in hand, and I went to walk in Banjo's labyrinth, where the dark man himself lay in wait for me.

10

My emotions were in an uproar as I walked into the woods that morning; I felt myself barely habitable. I wondered how Alex would react when she learned I had been in Diana's room. Would she misjudge my actions as readily as I had misjudged hers? For I thought I had done so and I was ashamed of myself. It comforted me to feel the trees closing in around me and know that I couldn't be seen. I wanted to hide myself away for a time.

I walked aimlessly, taking note of the turns I made after I had made them, and only vaguely aware of their sequence. I thought I knew the maze well enough and didn't expect to arrive at any juncture I had not previously explored. My head ached and my throat was tight, as if I were controlling a burst of anger. I stopped and squinted at the sun. The sky was cloudy and pale and the air was getting cooler by the minute. The leaves rustled on the trees. It had not rained in weeks and I welcomed the threat of it. I wondered if Diana and Alex were together in the kitchen, discussing my behavior.

A branch cracked behind me and I whirled around in the direction of the sound. There was a screen of leaves before me, but through it I could see a figure, a face, two brown eyes narrowed with consternation. I sucked my breath in sharply. This made him smile. He pushed aside the leaves that separated us and came confidently toward me. "Now you gone and found what you been looking for," he said.

"Have I?" I replied. I knew who he was and I thought that in some way I had been looking for him. I wanted and did not want the confirmation of my suspicions, and because his acquaintance had been forbidden me, I knew he held that confirmation.

But why, I thought, on that particular day? I had walked through his maze with impunity before, again and again, though not without some desire to see him. Today, when I did not see where I was going and did not care for even my own company, here he was. He stood before me, small, black, his gaze moody and superior, his manner irritable, like a tired trapper who has spent a day and snared, instead of mink, a possum. "Why don't you come along here with me and we can see what I can show you," he said. He turned ahead of me in the path and I followed him.

When the path ended twenty feet farther ahead, he pushed on through the foliage. He allowed the branches to snap back behind him; one scratched my arm and when I touched the spot I found blood. He muttered something inaudible, pushing another branch out of his way, stepping down and momentarily out of my sight. When I followed I found myself on a new path, wide and pleasant. The ground was strewn with pine needles, though the trees that bent over us were oak and cypress. Farther on, the path curved and ended in a small raised frame cottage with a screen porch. The walls were covered with ivy and the roof line sagged toward the front, but it was a neat, pleasant house and I was glad to see it for I longed to sit down.

Banjo went up the steps and threw the porch door open behind him, without looking back at me. I followed and found him sitting on a canvas chair at a card table. He motioned me into a second chair and brought out a jug similar to the one I had found on my first morning at Beaufort. "I believe you are a man who likes bourbon," he said.

I nodded. "And one who has had the pleasure of sampling yours before," I said. "For which I thank you now."

He nodded, then wiped his sweating forehead with his forearm. His skin was grainy and so black it was marvelous to see. His features were leonine—a long flat nose, small mouth, and wide heavy-lidded eyes that angled down toward his nose in an extraordinary fashion. He was small and compact and he moved gracefully, lifting the tumbler to his lips, closing his eyes as he swallowed, setting the drink down again. He gave me a long curious look; I felt he was comparing me to some standard. When he looked away I said, "Does my appearance interest you?"

"No," he said. "When I first saw you, you looks like someone else. But I see you don't look like him that much."

"I've been told that."

"Who told you that?"

"Collie. She said I looked like a man Diana and Alex had . . . cared for."

He snorted. "Did she tell you that?"

"Yes."

"How is Miss Collie doin'?" he asked. He was in control of the conversation and this pleased him.

"She's very well."

"What all did she tell you 'bout that man?"

"Only that Diana and Alex had quarreled over him."

He smiled to himself. "They did quarrel," he said, accenting the last word so that it was an understatement.

"Did you know him?"

"I only saw him one time and he was half dead. I think, considerin' the circumstances, I came to know him right well."

I didn't wish to draw him out further on this subject, as I thought him entirely too eager to tell me about it. I concentrated on my bourbon, then upon the line of clouds that rolled toward us above the trees. "It looks like quite a storm," I said.

"Sure," he said indifferently. He paused, then added, "What's the matter, man, they told you not to talk to me?"

"Diana asked me not to," I said.

"And you said you wouldn't."

"Why doesn't she want me to talk to you?" I asked.

He laughed. He had a loud self-effacing laugh that suggested great camaraderie and sympathy for its object. "Now, that I can't tell you," he said. "Those women are as scared of me as if I wanted to hurt them, which I don't. Though it ain't as if I couldn't, if I did, I will admit that."

"I thought you were afraid of them."

"Sure you did, man," he said. "Don't that just show you." He reached toward me to fill my glass.

I fought my inclination to give in and hear whatever it was he wanted to tell me. I found him too convincing already. I got up and stood at the edge of the porch.

"Are we near the center of your maze, here?" I asked.

His answer was aloof. "No, we outside it. You might say we was at the end of it."

"Or the beginning," I said.

"You suit yourself."

I returned to the table. "I thought I had it figured out," I said. "But I'm confused now."

"I can set you straight, if you want it."

I remembered Diana's terse reply when I had asked her what this man would tell me. He would lie, she had suggested, because he was useless to himself and to her. Then, abruptly, I recalled the way she had motioned Alex to her side the night before and the dull horror I had felt when she had discovered me in her room. These recollections left me with a sense of hopelessness, not powerful and heroic, like the hopelessness of loss, but flat, stale, airless, the despair of the everyday settling in after a brief flight of fancy, the end of a daydream or an elegant conversation.

"Tell me what you know about the man," I said. "Do you know his name?"

"His name was John, that's all they told me."

"How did you come to see him?"

He settled himself in his chair and filled his glass. "I was doing the gardens at the town house, it was ten years ago now, and one evening Miss Collie come running to my room in a bad state. She told me to take a key, what she gave me, and go out to this motel on the Airline Highway and to wipe the key off good and leave it in the door.

"I knew something was bad wrong right away. Collie ain't no woman given to panic. But I couldn't get much sense from her, so I told her to leave it to me and I would fix whatever it was. I would have done anything for her then. I loved her mother and I knew her from a baby. But not now. She's in the spell that Diana weaves on everyone what comes near her. Everyone but me." He paused and gave me an inquiring look. Was I, too, in the spell? As I didn't think I was, I felt no need to deny it. I nodded to him to go on.

"So I went on out there," he said. "When I was putting the key in the lock I heard a groaning sound, someone calling 'Help' but weak-like and faraway. So I opened the door and there I found this man lying in the bed. I went on up to him and saw he had a hole in his side big enough to stick two fingers in. He rolled his eyes up at me and then tried to look at his side. There was a big knife lyin' on the bed next to him what he'd pulled out of hisself, though how he did that I don't know." He paused, drank again. "It was Miss Alex's knife, so I wiped it on the bedsheet and put it in my coat.

"The man reached out to me. I pulled him up and pushed the pillows under him, trying to make him more comfortable. I said, 'Don't you know no better than to double-cross a woman who can throw knives like Miss Alex?' And he said, 'She didn't throw it. She stabbed me with her own hand.' Then he was crying and reached out again. I could look at the bed under him and know how long he'd be goin' on, 'cause there was so much blood it wouldn't soak in no more but stood on the sheet in a pool. Then he said again, 'She stabbed me,' like he couldn't believe it. And he clutched at his wound, weeping like a child."

He paused, giving me time to consider his story. Outside, it had begun to rain, softly, making a sound that hushed the air. I looked at Banjo and he looked back at me, with the hint of a smile at the corners of his mouth. I wanted to smash him. "Why should I believe this preposterous story?" I said.

"Why?" he repeated. "Why, because I'm sitting here, the living truth, and I've got no reason to lie. I don't know who you are. I don't even know which one of those women you in the tow of, though I expect it's Alex."

"What did you do then?" I said. "Did you stay with the man?"

"I did," he said. "I sat by that bed and watched him and I believe he was dead when I left. When I was going out I noticed something on the dresser, a white scarf. I knew it to be Miss Diana's, so I took it with me." He smiled. "Do you realize how bad them women botched this crime? If it hadn't been for me the police would of had Alex by the next day.

"So I took the scarf and wiped off everything I could think of so there wouldn't be no prints. Then I left."

"What did you say to Alex?"

"I didn't say nothing to her. I gave the knife and the scarf to Collie and I told her what I found. She didn't seem too surprised, so I figured she knew. The next morning I got called upstairs to see Miss Laura, and Alex and Diana was sitting in the room looking at me but they didn't speak. I looked Alex right in the face and she didn't so much as lower her eyes, she was that cool. Then Miss Laura asked me what I would most like to do in my life." He laughed, lifting his drink to his lips and eyeing me cheerfully over the glass. I couldn't help but smile back. "She asked me that," he said.

"Did you tell her the truth?" I asked.

"Shit, man, who knows that truth? I told her what I wanted that I knew she could give me. I said I wanted a house and a garden in the country, and a lifetime supply of good bourbon."

I laughed.

"And I said what I did not want was to have to talk to any fools or have anyone sneaking around asking me questions. After I said that, I looked at Alex and she gave me that smile that means she wants to cut your throat."

I looked away while that smile flooded through my consciousness like a perfume. I saw her as she had looked when she turned from me on the lawn, only hours earlier, and I thought, could she have done this thing, could she have killed a man? I was overcome by two convictions, one that she could not have done it, the second that she had certainly done it. I felt I had evidence for either conclusion.

"That's how I come to be here," Banjo concluded. "But I stays away from those women 'cause I seen the grief they can cause."

I sat looking at my drink, trying to sort out my impressions. Banjo lapsed into silence and moved only to refill our glasses. In spite of the unpleasant story he had told me I didn't wish to leave him. It had been some time since I'd had the company of another man and I found that I was enjoying it. I felt I could relax and drink myself into oblivion if I wished and it wouldn't matter how dull I became or whether I had anything intelligent to say. I suspected that Banjo knew a good deal about Alex and Diana, and if this knowledge caused him to tell a defamatory lie about them, then it would be worth my time to find out why. If it was not a lie, then he could only tell me what couldn't be altered.

"Do you like Alex?" I said after a while.

"I remember the first day she came to the house," he said, raising his eyebrows. "She's a child to me."

"Then you do like her."

"I knows her," he said. "I saw everything that changed her and sometimes I knew it before she did."

"She was close to you?"

"She never cared for me, but I took an interest in her. Because she was . . ." He paused. "From the start she was like she is now. You can't touch her no way. No one gets near her."

I looked away. The rain was steady and strong now, with startling flashes of lightning and dull distant thunder, like the recollection of pain.

"I don't believe," he said, "even Diana has her confidence. I believe she has never shared her confidence."

I found myself gazing at his quizzical face. Did he want me to verify this proposition? "What about Diana?" I asked.

"Diana?" he said. "Now she is a problem."

"To you?"

"Not to me." He laughed. "Not to me. She don't bother me. But if I let her, she would. She want everybody to serve her. That's all she wants." He leaned toward me across the table. "It always seemed to me that she passed for being smart and sensible, while Alex was always made out to be wild, when the truth was it's the other way 'round."

"You think Diana is wild?" I said.

"I think she's mean," he replied. "Maybe Alex did drive that knife into that man, but he was dead when he walked out that front door with Diana and she knew it. She knew Alex would kill him. She knows what folks will do. She can't resist trying out what she knows; she's testing everybody that loves her, and then she's always disappointed because . . . she knew all along."

I couldn't make out the sense of these observations, so I made no comment. Banjo got up and flicked on a ceiling fan. "It's on to lunchtime," he said. "I got some cold fried chicken in here." He pointed to the dark interior of his cottage. "And some potato salad and beans. I bet you ain't had a thing but greens since you come here."

I looked at the rain and wondered what they would think at the house. I felt certain Alex would guess the truth. "That sounds good," I said.

Banjo disappeared inside, came out with a bowl of ice, then went inside again without speaking. I felt weak and hot and my throat was closed tight around a spot of irritation at the back of my tongue. I decided to eat and then go back as soon as the rain let up.

But the rain didn't let up, nor did Banjo's supply of bourbon. My consciousness of the passage of time expanded with each glass I drank and it was late afternoon before it occurred to me that I should return to the house, rain or no rain. Banjo didn't want me to go; he showed me everything he had that might interest me and held my imagination for a long time with drawings of the successive stages of his labyrinth. It had started, I learned, quite simply, two concentric circles with adjoining spokes, but gradually, a bush planted here, a slice of the machete there, the sinuous and misleading curves, the dead ends, the abrupt turns, had evolved. He explained that when he wished to cut off a path he let it alone for a month and it returned to its natural impenetrable shape. The effort he expended in maintaining it and in constantly changing it impressed me, for it must have been considerable. He was proud of it and pleased with my interest. "I usually see you in the morning," he said, "when you running around." He laughed. "Sometimes I'm just a few feet away."

I told him I had spotted him only once, on my first visit.

"I knew that," he said. "I was as scared as you was. I thought you was that dead man come back to get even with me."

I smiled. "In a way, I think I am," I said. His eyes widened. His story was true, I thought then. I wanted to put as much distance between myself and that thought as I could.

"I've got to leave now," I said abruptly. "I have to get back." I got to my feet and staggered forward. When I pressed my arm to my forehead I found it unnaturally hot. I turned to look at Banjo, who smiled at me benignly over a pile of gnawed chicken bones, and I wondered if he had poisoned me. But my throat had been sore since morning, I told myself.

"Can you find your way, man?" he inquired, making no gesture to help me, though I stood clinging to the door frame, clearly helpless.

"I believe I'm ill," I said.

"You just drunk too much. If you walk, your head will clear."

"That may be true," I said. I stepped off the porch and into the rain, which cooled me and made my thought processes momentarily crystalline. I was surprised to discover, not that I believed Alex had killed a man, but that I believed if she had, it was because she had been forced to. I did not think her culpable. The man behind me had described the scene she left, what of the scene she had found? Excuses for her leaped to my mind and every one was a good one. I was ready to go to court for her. The important thing was this, I didn't care if she had killed one man or a dozen men, she was not changed for me. I had a strong desire to be near her.

I took a few more steps away from the house. Rain dripped down my neck and back. Banjo called out behind me, "You think you goin' to find your way?" It was a challenge.

I stopped and turned to him. "Through those bushes there," I said, gesturing toward the end of the path.

"And then you'll be right where I found you," he replied.

"I can find my way from there," I said, turning away. I stumbled ahead and climbed the small embankment that separated his house from the maze. I took a right at the first fork and hurried on down the path, burning with fever, dulled with drink, and curiously convinced that if I followed my intuitions I would shortly find myself on the sloping green lawn of Beaufort.

I must pause in my narration to explain that after this point my memory is not clear. Or rather it is strikingly clear, full of vivid flashes that catch me when I do not expect them, like lightning. All I can relate is the sequence of these flashes; much was lost in between and, I fear, some of my recollections only serve to heighten my distrust of my own memory.

I was soon lost, though I never believed it. The sky, which was none too light when I set out, was dark, overcast, starless, and moonless. It rolled over me like a blanket. I remember thinking that I would lie down for a few moments and try to collect my wits. I stretched out in the path, oblivious to thistles, spiders, ants, and an instant sheet of mosquitoes. I was fascinated by the heat my body generated and continually touched myself—my head, my neck, my armpits —to determine if I was better or worse. I fell asleep, I woke up, I attempted to call out, though I expected no one to hear me. My voice was gone. I tried to convince myself that Banjo had poisoned me and that I would soon be dead. But I didn't believe I was dying, I couldn't believe it was that simple. I thought of Alex; I longed for her with a pure physical longing, I ached for her. When I closed my eyes the earth stopped spinning beneath me and I felt her with me, above me, beneath me, her limbs wrapped tightly about me, but when I opened them again it was like being thrust apart from her. Parts of my body quivered with the recollection of her. I felt like a victim of a wholesale amputation; vital parts of me were missing but I still experienced them, responded to them. I wanted her and my not having her made me so sorry for myself that I wept. After a long time, and great confusion of mind, I became aware of some light in the distance. The wood appeared to be on fire. I could see the flames leaping up over the high grass and I could smell kerosene. I got to my knees and tried to crawl away from it, but I was weak and my legs seemed to slip out from under me. Then I heard a voice I scarcely recognized, raised as I had never heard it, in furious agitation. "We were fools to trust him," Diana said. "If he's dead, so much the better for us."

I whirled in my tracks and threw myself into a dark body. "Son-of-a-bitch," the body said. "Here he is and damned if he ain't alive."

It was Collie. She bent over me, bringing the torch she carried down so that she could see my face. "Lord," she said, "these insects had a meal off of him."

Another torch, another face. Diana scowled at me. "Damn," she said. "We ought to leave him out here."

Alex's face, white and cold, looked down over her shoulder. I felt a sharp pain in my rib cage and recoiled from it, shocked speechless. One of them had kicked me.

"Bastard," Diana said indifferently.

I believe I rolled toward them until I contacted a pair of legs and I believe I sunk my teeth into one of those legs as hard as I could. There was a cry, a blow across my back. Diana laughed. "He's vicious," she said.

"Let's take him back," Alex said.

They were bending over me and there was a strong smell of kerosene and the light from their torches blinded me. I tried to get to my feet but I was helpless. I believe Collie and Alex took me by the shoulders and Diana took my feet. I felt my body being lifted and carried along and I was relieved to feel air moving over me and to hear, instead of the roar of mosquitoes, the fluttery hissing sound of burning.

11

For some time it was as if my eyes had turned inward. I was hot, I sweated, my skin cooled, then burned afresh. I had little consciousness of externals. Once I saw a spoon near my ear and I concluded I was being fed. Another time I knocked a glass of water off the nightstand and I saw the clear liquid fragmenting in the air.

The first time I opened my eyes and saw Alex's back, she was leaving the room. I called her name and she turned to me, floated toward me, one hand raised before her as if she would strike me. But I didn't care and reached out to her. Then she was gone.

I opened my eyes again and saw Collie sitting near the bed, sewing. I watched her dark fingers flicking the silver needle through the cloth; it glittered and turned dull and disappeared. At length I felt her eyes on mine and I looked at her face, bent over her work, gazing down at me as if she was surprised to find me there. "Can you hear me?" she said.

I nodded.

"Too bad I don't have nothing to say to you." She returned her attention to her sewing.

I looked down at myself and saw my chest rising and falling beneath the sheet. My skin was prickly and hot and I could feel my own outline radiating a field of heat down to my toes. I was overcome with a desire to hear my own voice; would it be there if I tried to use it? I said "Alex," out loud. It sounded a little high but it was my voice.

Collie looked down at me. "God knows what you done to her," she said. "She ain't herself."

I felt myself drifting away from this response, as if it were a wave that carried me.

I woke up. I was alone in the room and it was dark. I was soaked with sweat; the sheets could have been wrung out. I got out of bed and staggered to the window. I thought, "This must mean I'm getting better." I looked out over the lawn and saw the sweet-olive trees, their bark pale in soft moonlight. Something about this view excited me. I went to Alex's door and knelt down, pressing my ear, then my eye against the keyhole. I had a terrific erection, rising slowly, steadily, standing up for me like an old friend. "Good," I thought. "I'll get well now." I stood up too quickly and threw out my hands before me, but I don't remember in which direction I fell.

The room was half dark; someone was talking. "If we bring a doctor into this it'll just mean a lot of questions." I could make out two women, Diana and Alex, sitting on the couch. Collie sat in the chair, her back to me. "There ain't gonna be much a doctor can do for him anyhow," she said.

I tried to speak, to say I wanted a doctor, but no sound came out.

Alex leaned forward, her elbows resting on her knees. "If he dies, how will we dispose of him?"

I was aware of another presence in the room, very near me, standing next to the bed, looking down at me, his dark face solemn and speculative. "I'll take care of that for you," he said. He leaned over me and put his cold hand on my arm and I recoiled from it. "Banjo," I said, but I couldn't make myself heard. Then, as his face came closer and closer to me, the color in it drained away until his skin was very white and his hair was whiter still. "How long has he been like this?" he asked, looking to Diana.

"He's always been like this," she replied.

I tried to pull myself up to get my hands on the man, whoever he was, and as I did so, I saw his hand moving toward my arm, and closed in his grip, the unexpected glinting of a needle. I heard Alex say, "It's not as if anyone will look for him." Then terror and a fierce yearning for sleep consumed me.

I woke up. Alex stood next to my bed but she wasn't looking at me. Her face was averted, as if she were listening to a sound from far away. Then she turned to me and put her hands over my temples, bending over me so that I inhaled the perfume of her breasts. I reached out to her.

"You're awake?" she whispered. "You know who I am?"

I drew her down to me, kissing whatever came near my mouth, her breasts, her shoulders, her neck.

"You're so hot," she said. "You're burning up."

I pushed her gown aside and caressed her cool skin. I did feel I was burning but the fire gave me a supernatural strength. It was as if I could quench the flames by plunging myself into her cool liquid flesh.

"Can you do this?" she inquired.

"I need water," I said, surprised to hear my own voice.

She drew away and returned with a glass of water. I propped myself up on one elbow and drank deeply; as I did she caressed me nervously, her hands darting across my skin, impatient, greedy. I finished my drink and set the glass on the nightstand.

"I'm sorry," she said, sinking down upon me. "I know you're ill."

I stroked her smooth strong back and cooled my burning mouth upon her breasts. She was very still, tensed, her back arched up so that her hips were forced down. She sighed. "You're so hot," she said.

"I know it," I replied.

She moved her hips in a circular pattern and I pressed the heels of my hands into her buttocks, holding her fast. My erection was like a torch, it consumed the air, and I felt the energy expended in burning it was draining me from the head down. I slipped inside her without the aid of hands. She moaned softly and threw her head back, savoring every inch gained between us. Then she let her head fall forward on her chest and I saw that she was weeping. She didn't stop but kept moving over me slowly, her breath catching in her throat while tears streamed down her cheeks and fell on my stomach and chest, where they streaked down my sides like burning oil.

"Alex," I said. "What is it?" I tried to pull her head down so that I could comfort her, but she held her arms stiff and wouldn't bend to me. Then she opened her eyes and gazed at me through tears. She looked at me from such a distance, through so much fire, that I felt I had never seen her before. The motion of her hips was slow, regular, circular. I felt as if we were being lifted in the air and turned upright, so that we whirled in a column together, our heads above the atmosphere. I could hear music. I realized that it was Diana's piano and that I had heard the sad languor of her song before. It was too slow, I thought, and not in keeping with the activity of our bodies, and yet it was more touching for that. It was pitiful to burn and drive and lose myself in Alex's dark eyes while these sounds of the purest serenity cleansed the air.

I had a peculiar idea. It must be, I thought, as shocking to be entered as to enter. But in exactly the opposite way, requiring a reverse of every sentiment, every inclination, so that for every "let me," there was a "please," for every "you must," an "I will." And then, at least for us, the balance was perfect.

It was perfect but I was fast becoming delirious. Alex collapsed across me and fell to sucking at my fingers like an infant.

"Are you trying to kill me?" I said.

She rolled off me, turned her back to me. "It must seem that way to you," she said.

"I mean it literally. Do you know if I'm dying?"

"No," she said. "I don't know. I don't think so."

"How long have I been like this?"

"A week."

I took a handful of her hair and pulled it, trying to make her turn to me. "Have you missed me?"

"I've been watching you every minute," she said, pulling farther away so that some of the strands came loose and remained twisted in my fingers. I felt myself drifting away. "I wasn't finished," I protested, begging to be restored. "I wasn't done yet."

I kept my eyes closed for a few moments. I could feel sunlight on their lids and hear the sound of birds singing. There was even a pleasant odor of mowed grass in the air. I knew at once that my fever was gone, but still I was reluctant to see where I was because I feared the white-hot confusion, the sensory uncertainty that had greeted me the last few times I had looked out. I counted to ten and, hoping for the best, opened my eyes.

I was looking into Diana's perfect features. Her nostrils flared slightly as she pulled away. "I beg your pardon," she said. "Somehow I knew you were conscious."

I looked about the room. Everything was clear and calm; the red edge around my vision was gone. I allowed my gaze to wander over the familiar furniture and it struck me as odd that I thought of this pleasant room as my own. My eyes settled at last upon Diana, who had pulled a chair up to my bed and seated herself next to me.

"How do you feel?" she said.

"Weak. But better. Much better."

"I don't believe you were seriously ill, but your fever was very high and nothing we did seemed to help."

"To what do you attribute your success?" I asked, leaning

toward her. She sat with her hands folded over her stomach, which, I noticed, had pushed out to a preposterous size, so that she appeared to be leaning upon a large ball hidden in the folds of her dress. "I suppose it was only a matter of time."

"How long?"

"Two weeks," she said. "Two weeks exactly."

"Did Banjo help you find me?"

She laughed. "No."

"He knew I wouldn't find my way out."

"I believe I warned you of such an eventuality."

"You only told me he was a liar."

She adjusted her skirt across her knees. "I'm sure he proved to be that, too."

"He did tell me a fantastic story."

"Which you believed?"

"I did. I could believe it."

"What exactly did he say?"

"He said that Alex killed that man."

She smiled. "She wanted to," she said, "but she didn't."

My head ached. I was aware of myself as a perspiring bed-worn body I wanted to get away from. I sat up. The room spun before me; then my focus cleared. "I want to talk about this," I said, "but I think I should bathe first. If I can get out of this bed."

Diana rose to her impressive height and assisted me to my feet. My arm brushed against the taut skin of her stomach. "You look as if it can't be much longer," I said.

"A few weeks."

I staggered against her, surprised at the strength with which she held my arm and resettled my balance. We reached the bathroom and I sat on the marble edge of the tub.

"Will you need help in here?" she asked.

I felt the sight of me would offend her delicacy and insisted that I could manage alone.

"Shall I send Alex to you?" she asked.

"No. If you could wait. I'd like to talk to you."

She went out, closing the door behind her. "I'll wait in here," she said.

I sat alone in the bathroom and struggled with the problem of undressing myself. I was wearing pajamas I didn't recognize though I was sure they were to Alex's taste.

Where was she? My desire to see her made me determined to regain my equilibrium. I bathed quickly and thoroughly, brushed my teeth, and put on my robe, which was hanging on the door where I had left it two weeks ago. I thought of how I had gone out that morning, worrying that perhaps my beloved was not all my own. Now I had to consider the possibility that she was a murderess. Of the two, I found the latter easier to bear.

When I returned to my room Diana was sitting on the chair next to my bed, her arms crossed, her legs slightly apart. I threw myself down on the couch. "I can't get back in that bed," I said.

She smiled. "Banjo is gone," she said.

"You threw him out?"

"No. I would never do that. He has a sinecure here. He just left, of his own accord."

"How do you know he's gone? Have you looked for him?"

"You know how eager nature is around here," she said, indicating the window with a lift of her chin. "If you leave it alone for two weeks, it's as if you were never there."

"His maze is gone?"

"You can still make it out. Collie went in and looked in his house but she didn't see him."

"Perhaps he's hiding."

"I suppose that's possible," she said. "He's certainly crazy enough to do something like that. But I'm inclined to believe that he has left us."

"It's just as well," I said. "If I could find him I'd probably try to kill him."

She smiled, looking away from me.

"I want you to tell me what happened that night," I said. "I want to know what happened to that man."

"I don't know what happened to him," she said. "I never saw him again."

"But Alex didn't kill him?"

She shook her head, causing a strand of hair to come loose and slip down her long neck. "It's an unpleasant story," she said. "And it's painful to me to recall it."

"But you will?"

"I will only because I think you deserve to know."

"I think I need to know," I said.

She folded and unfolded the lap of her skirt, like a child. "Have you ever been in love with someone about whom you were completely mistaken?"

"Persistently," I said.

She ignored my joke. "I don't know how I could have been so foolish. Alex tried to warn me but I thought she was angry because he had lost interest in her."

"What did she say?"

"She said she was finished with him. And that she thought he was too dangerous for me." Her eyes met mine and she sighed. "That only made me more interested in him. I didn't know she meant it literally."

"That he was dangerous."

"He was ill, I guess. Though I believe the kind of illness he had is becoming widespread."

I said nothing and she continued.

"He had flirted with me a lot, usually while he was waiting for Alex, and I found him attractive in a peculiar way, the way some animals are attractive. I was stunned when he was near me, hypnotized. One night he had a quarrel with Alex in the house. I heard them shouting but I couldn't make out what they were saying. Alex went to her room and slammed the door. When I went down to see her I found him sitting at the foot of the stairs."

"Waiting for you?"

"Or for Alex. I'll never know. I asked him what the quarrel was about and he said it was about me, because Alex knew he was interested in me and she wouldn't stand for it.

"I guess I knew that wasn't true. Alex had already told me she intended to ditch him. But he kept talking, he was very clever and told me I was to go with him at once, before Alex could do anything about it." She paused and rubbed her lips against the back of her hand.

"It's hard for me to talk about this. I've spent such a long time trying to forget it."

Again I kept quiet and she continued.

"He was very persuasive and the end of it was that I went with him. He drove me to a motel on the Airline Highway— it was somewhat run-down—and took me to a room. I'd never been in such a place before. He already had the room key.

"I sat on the bed and he came to me and undressed me. He was gentle but he said a few things that rather shocked me." She paused again and turned her eyes upon me, with the look of someone who is about to burst into hysterical laughter.

"I should have known," she said. "I should have gone then. I knew something was going wrong. But I was so naïve. I kept thinking that I would go just a little further, just a little longer, to see what would happen, I suppose. I couldn't believe anyone would really want to make me unhappy. Most of the men I'd known had been somewhat awed by me. I'd always had everything just as I wanted it. I think I thought my beauty made me inviolate." She laughed and her cheeks flushed with color. I thought her very beautiful.

"I let him go as far as to bind my hands behind my back. He had a suitcase in the room and he took the rope from it. When he opened it I saw two cameras, one was a movie camera, and my heart sank. I tried hard not to panic. I tried to think of what Alex would do.

"That was what saved me. Alex always knows what to do. She can coerce anyone. I told him that I wasn't unwilling to indulge his fantasies but that I was tired and thirsty and could do with some bourbon. I thought he would be more suspicious than he was. He agreed to go out, on the condition that I was to await his return tied to the bed. I would have done anything to get him out of the room and I decided to worry about how I would escape once he was gone. So I let him tape my mouth and he tied my wrists to the side rail of the bed.

"When he went out I went crazy. I struggled so violently that the rope cut my wrists. I moved the bed clear across the room and tried to get the door open with my feet. I have no memory of having done this. I was mad with fear and I believed that if I didn't escape he would probably come back and kill me.

"I heard footsteps outside the door and I thought it was him, I thought I was dead. Then a key turned in the lock and the door was forced open against me. I was wedged between the bed and the door. I saw a clenched hand and a knife gleaming in the fist. When I saw the blade I knew I was saved. It was Alex's knife.

"She cut me loose and helped me get dressed. I was so weak with relief I could barely stand. She was angry with me but she was more angry with herself. She said she had known this was going to happen but had convinced herself she was being hysterical. We were both frantic to get away, and later, when we got home, I discovered I'd left a scarf behind. Alex had left her knife and kept the key to the room.

"I don't know what we thought he could have done to us but I was afraid of any kind of scandal then." She paused and considered her unborn child. "Though I don't care much now. As you can see."

"That's a different kind of scandal," I observed.

"I suppose so," she said. "Anyway, I was anxious, so Alex consulted Collie, who, I believe, spoke to Banjo. The next day Alex had her knife and I received my scarf."

"And Banjo retired."

"That was something my mother did. I never knew how much she knew. We weren't in the habit of confiding in one another."

"And what happened to the man?"

"Mercifully, we never heard from him again."

We were quiet for a moment. Diana was clearly distressed by what she had told me.

"The first day I was here, you said he was dead."

She looked up, then returned her gaze to the floor. "He is, as far as I'm concerned."

I persisted. "Banjo told me he found him dead in that motel room."

"Did he?" she said. She was unable to give me her full attention. "That would be just as well."

I squirmed among the couch cushions in search of a comfortable position. I was lightheaded again and confused. I could think of nothing but Alex.

"I don't doubt," Diana continued, "that I've overreacted to the incident. It's been years now, but when I think of it, when I talk about it, all the horror I felt then comes back." She swallowed uncomfortably. "It makes me nauseous still."

"And distrustful of all men," I speculated.

"Not so much as you might think. For example, I trust you. I feel a certain affection for you, and you bear a superficial resemblance to this man. I don't fear that what happened will happen again. It's only as if everything were spoiled somehow. Soured. Everything. Every pleasure." She fell silent and I noticed that her hands were closed in tight fists.

"That explains," I said, "why you choose to live as you do."

"Many people would prefer to live out of society if they could. Look at yourself."

"But I was never comfortable there, not born to it, as you were. I was in no way an ornament to it." I laughed.

She smiled. "That describes what I was. An ornament. Brittle as glass. No. I'm happier as I am."

"Still," I said. "I always think beautiful women should be seen."

She laughed. "For what?" she said. "So that they may inspire rage and envy?"

"So that they may be admired."

"Do you really believe beauty is still admired?"

"I believe it always has been."

"Oh, Claude," she said, as if addressing a child. "Beauty is despised in every quarter. I should know. I'm beautiful. What happened was only the proof of a case I'd seen good evidence for. All I've ever inspired in men is a desire to bring me down, make me weak, pervert me, or sometimes they simply wish to cut me to ribbons."

I was silent.

"Fortunately, I find a certain reward in my own beauty." She paused. "That sounds egotistical, but it's true, I can't deny it. Somedays, being beautiful is enough. That's why I wanted a child, to share that with. There's not much chance of his being anything but beautiful. And even if he isn't, I hope to impart to him some sense of what beauty deserves, in all its manifestations."

"But how will he survive in the world?"

"I won't allow him in it. Not for a minute. Oh, I suppose if he wants to leave me when he's older I'll have to let him go. But no schools. No hate. No envy, no greed."

"You'll teach him yourself?"

"I was wondering if you could teach him math. I know very little about it, but I believe it to be important. I understand that there is even some pleasure to be had in the study of it."

I was surprised to learn that she had manufactured a future for me. "Diana," I said, "this is a strange idea, though I'm sure you know it's not original with you."

"I don't care where it came from. It's my idea now. I won't go live among murderers and robbers and perverts again."

I had never heard her speak in this way. "You have no hope for the future?"

"The future is for madmen. There's a great future in the world for madness and anarchy and hate. It gets worse every year. I haven't even lived very long but I've felt the rise in the curve myself."

"I thought I was pessimistic," I said. "But I don't see things this bleakly."

She smiled. "The world hasn't seen pessimism like what it's bred in the last generation. You and your group are always moaning about the state of the world, but you don't know the half of it because you remember, or you say you remember, something different. I know, Alex knows, we have been born into the desert and we know there is nothing but desert on every side and it gets bigger every year. It can't be changed and it doesn't even matter whose fault it is. The end of it is despair, it's despair, look around you. Even the artists don't try to fake it any more. Beauty simply excites their contempt."

"If you believe that," I said, "I can't see why you would want to bring another person into the desert."

She sighed and rubbed her forehead with her hand. "I suppose I shouldn't have. But I can't help but hope I'm wrong."

"And the world is not insane."

"And that my poor child will find me insane and forgive me for it."

"Do you think you are?"

"Oh God." She laughed. "I hope so. If it's not that, it's prescience, which would be worse."

As I formulated my reply to this (for I felt obliged to convince her that she was saner than she knew, in spite of my discovery that she was less sane than I had suspected), there was a knock at the door and suddenly, unexpectedly, Alex stood before me.

She was dressed all in black and her mouth was stretched into a smile of embarrassed pleasure. For a moment she didn't speak but filled the room with electric excitement so that Diana rose to her feet and smoothed her hair and I sat up on my couch, feeling as strong and sound as I had ever felt.

"You're out of bed?" she said.

"I've returned to the living."

Diana looked from Alex to me and back again. "We've concluded a bizarre conversation," she said. "And I was just leaving to look for you." She passed Alex, who had not moved, and went out, closing the door quietly behind her.

Alex crossed to me quickly and sat down beside me. I took her hands in my own. "I'm delighted to see you," I said.

She looked away at my disheveled bed. "It's as if you'd been away and someone else was in your place."

"Did I say anything I shouldn't have?"

She smiled, still gazing at the sheets as if she saw me lying there, tossing amid my heated fantasies. "You were terrific," she said. "I can't stand sick people but I was mad for you."

"I remember an evening visit."

She looked at me, blushing to the roots of her hair. "You do remember." Then, abruptly, she covered her face with her hands and collapsed across my lap, weeping as if her heart would break.

12

It has been my experience that the last version of a story is the one that vibrates in the imagination with the ring of truth. Banjo's story, with its unpleasant implications, slipped from my thoughts and I found Diana's version more satisfying. In fact, the two stories didn't necessarily contradict one another. It was possible that someone else had killed the man, using Alex's knife, after she and Diana had fled. I believed Diana for another reason as well, because it explained her contempt for a world that had really done her very little harm.

In a week's time I was recovered and fell gladly back into my old routine. Alex treated me as if she had nearly lost me and had sensed what that loss would have meant. She was, by turns, excessively considerate and inexplicably petulant. I suspected that part of this moodiness was caused by my growing friendship with Diana, who sought me out to talk about her impending delivery as if she thought I might know something about it.

I knew nothing and frankly told her so, but I was interested in her state of mind, which struck me as remarkably calm, considering what was in store for her. I didn't guess then what she had in store for me.

It happened about ten days after my recovery. Diana was overdue and was seeing her physician every three days. On the last two visits he had assured her that she wouldn't make the next and endeavored to convince her that she should move into town so that he might tend her more closely. She had never liked him, and as the time grew nearer, the rift between them widened. Diana wanted the baby delivered in a specific way, without anesthesia, without bright lights, without noise. (She explained all this, and her reasons for wanting it, on one of our many trips across the lake together.) Her doctor, a man of my generation, who believed he had pulled enough babies into the world to know how it should be done, was having none of it. She had attended childbirth classes without his permission. I recalled the letter she had written Alex, in which she had suggested that she and Collie would help her deliver the child, and I wondered if she didn't plan simply to stay away from this insensitive man when the time came. She continued to see him, she said, only to make sure everything was progressing normally. So far, he told her, it was.

We had crossed the lake in the morning and I was lying on the deck waiting for her return. I was agitated because, for the first time, Diana had consented to make the trip below deck in the cabin and, halfway across, she had asked me to take the wheel. She didn't, however, appear to be in any pain, and as I knew little about how childbirth begins, I thought perhaps she was only very tired. She had driven off in the sports car she left at the yacht harbor, saying only that she would return immediately after her visit. As the doctor's office was a few minutes away, I didn't expect to wait very long.

I had just begun to speculate on why she might be late when I heard quick footsteps on the pier and looked up to see her approaching. She smiled at me and swung down over the side of the boat with unexpected grace.

"What did he say?" I asked, sitting up and shading my eyes against the sun.

"I'm fine," she said. "Three more days. Let's go home." She went into the cabin and I followed her. "Will you drive?" she said. I took my place behind the wheel and she sat down at the table, stretching her long arms across it and resting her head against the smooth wooden surface.

"Are you sure you're all right?" I said.

She didn't answer and when I turned to see her she had pressed her forehead against the table and she was breathing very slowly, her eyes and mouth half open. Then she sat up and gave me a questioning look. "Sure," she said. "Let's go."

I slowly backed the boat out of the slip and we moved out of the harbor. It was late in the afternoon and I guessed that we would make it back to Beaufort by dark. I was anxious to return, for Alex had been curt with me at breakfast and I wanted to find out why. I imagined that she didn't like my spending the day with Diana, but as she would never admit to such a thing, I was left to my suspicions.

"Did you have any luck with him?" I asked, as I increased the engine speed and headed out across the water.

"With my doctor?" she said. "No. He'd tie my hands and feet and pry the baby out with a crowbar if I gave him the chance."

"Which you won't," I said.

"Not a chance," she replied. Again she put her head down on the table and breathed in slowly, audibly. I concentrated on my steering and we went out for perhaps ten miles without speaking.

Only very gradually did I realize that there was something wrong with the boat. First the motor missed a few times. When I reduced speed, it ran normally. Then, without any pressure from me, the engine sped up abruptly, then slowed again. Diana looked up and I gave her a quizzical look. "It's nothing I'm doing," I said.

Her face was extraordinarily pale. "Christ," she said, looking out over the water. It was a calm, hot day and there wasn't another boat in sight. The sun was going down already. "What do you think it is?"

"I don't know," I said. The motor missed, missed again, then sputtered. We went on like this for half a mile, then with a last spurt of power the motor died. When I tried to start it again, it turned over but wouldn't catch. Diana looked at me, wide-eyed, as it ground to a stop. A second try produced nothing. "It's dead," I said.

She smiled. "Will you try to fix it?"

"I'll take a look at it," I said. "It might be water in the fuel line. I don't know."

I went to the back of the boat and opened the doors that concealed the motor. I knew little about boat motors and I was surprised at the size of the one that confronted me. It was jammed so tightly into its compartment it looked as if it would have to be completely removed to change a spark plug. The fuel tanks were not, as I had hoped, separate, but ran underneath the works. I checked the oil and a few connections but nothing appeared to be amiss. I closed the doors and went back to the cabin, where I found Diana lying on her side on the leather couch. "Are you all right?" I said.

She sat up and laid her hands along either side of her stomach as if she meant to present it to me. "What's wrong with the motor?" she said.

"I don't know. I can't fix it. It's packed in there as tight . . ."

"As this baby," she finished for me. "I'm afraid I have some startling news for you."

"Diana," I said.

"I'm in labor," she said.

"Are you sure?"

She smiled at me, child that I was. "Yes, I'm sure. I was dilated three centimeters at the doctor's. When I left him I told him I was going to the hospital, but he said it would probably be another six or eight hours, so I decided to go home and let Alex help me."

I glanced frantically around the cabin. "Don't you have some kind of radio in this thing."

"Nothing," she said. "But we can boil all the water we want if it'll make you feel better. And there are plenty of sheets and blankets." She stopped and sucked in her breath quickly, then began breathing very slowly as she had done before. After a minute she stopped. "I'm going to give you a crash course," she said. "I'll need your help and when I get further along I may not be able to tell you what to do."

"Surely someone will find us in time," I said.

"I've no idea," she said.

"You're right. Tell me what to do."

She started to speak, then stopped and took a deep breath. For a few moments she breathed deeply and slowly. Then, blowing out harshly, she turned her attention to me. "That was a contraction," she said. "I'm having them about three minutes apart now. I want you to time the next one. When it starts I'll nod my head and take a deep breath. Okay?"

I glanced at my watch. "Sure," I said.

"That part will be easy, but what I'll really need you for is to tell me when I'm fully dilated so I won't be trying to push too soon."

"How will I do that?"

She blushed and looked away.

"Diana," I said. "I don't think you're going to be able to be shy, and I assure you I won't be put off by anything. Honestly, I'm excited by the prospect."

"You're not afraid."

"I'm terrified," I said. "But not of you."

"You'll have to put your fingers inside and feel the edge of the cervix. There's supposed to be a rim you can feel. It has to be this wide"—she made a circle with her thumbs and third fingers—"before I'm ready."

"Exactly that wide," I said. I imitated her circle with my own and we held our hands together so that I could alter mine to fit hers.

"Yes," she said.

"What about cutting the cord?" I asked. It was the only thing I knew I would have to do.

"I think that will be the least of our worries. You may have to cut me."

I felt a weakness in my stomach, but I was determined not to frighten Diana. Before I could answer, she nodded her head quickly and took in a long breath. I watched the second hand on my watch until she nodded again and stopped.

"How long was it?" she said.

"Forty seconds. Did it hurt?"

"Not much. Not yet. It'll be a while, I think."

"Shall we set up a bed of some kind?"

"I think the table will be best. I'll get some sheets to put on it. Then I want to take a shower before it gets much further along."

"Is that wise?"

"Yes. I'm supposed to. You should get yourself as clean as you can, too, and we'll have to scrub the table down and boil the straight razor."

"The straight razor?" I said.

"It's in the bathroom. I'll go take my shower now and bring it with me when I come back."

She had another contraction, fifty-five seconds, before she left. While she was gone I scrubbed the table with dishwashing soap, and water which I heated on the hot plate. I was continually looking out the window at the darkening sky and the empty horizon. I believed another boat would come along soon and we would be rushed back to New Orleans, where Diana's doctor would be waiting, outraged but competent. My faith in this eventuality kept me calm, and I trusted that if we were not discovered before the baby was born I would not, until the last moment, give up this confidence.

Diana came out wrapped in a beach towel. She stood in the small door of the shower and gazed at me with an air of consummate distraction.

"Are you all right?" I said.

"The waters broke," she said. "I think things are speeding up." She crossed the small cabin and climbed up on the table. "Would you get some sheets, they're under that seat," she said, gesturing toward the opposite couch. "Then come sit here and I'll try to explain as much as I know."

I did as she suggested, and for the next half hour, she advised me between contractions. I timed these; they were even and she seemed to be absorbed by them but not in severe pain. I thought, if it got no worse, we would do well.

The lights were on in the cabin and as it grew dark outside it was impossible to see through the windows. A vessel approaching us would, I thought, see us clearly, and what they would make of it I couldn't guess. Diana held my hand calmly in her own, her head resting on a cushion, her great swollen body rising like a hill beneath the sheet, stretched across a table that was too small. The contractions were becoming stronger and closer together. She gripped my arm at the beginning of one and gulped frantically at the air like a fish out of water. Her eyes met mine but I didn't feel that she saw me. "Relax," I said. "Don't tense up. Relax your legs." I touched her legs, which she had drawn up beneath her. Still she clung to me and color drained from her face. I touched her forehead, stroked her damp hair away from her cheeks. The peak of the contraction passed and she began to relax. "That was awful," she said when she could speak again. Her voice was so faint I had to lean over to her to make out what she said. "I couldn't find the beginning. Before I knew what to do, it was on me."

"Don't talk," I said. She opened her mouth as if to speak, then sucked in her breath again and reverted to slow deep breathing. In the midst of this contraction she broke into rapid panting. I ran my hand across her stomach and felt the rock-hardness of her uterus, as powerful a muscle as any that exists. The panting seemed to help. When this contraction was over, she breathed slowly, her eyes fixed absently on my face. I pressed a damp cloth to her lips and she sucked it wearily.

In this way, without speaking, because she couldn't speak and because I felt myself so occupied there was no need to speak, we passed three hours, one minute at a time. On several occasions, at the end of a contraction, she discharged large quantities of blood. This disturbed her, though she expressed her concern only with a weak request that I take the sheets away. Her self-absorption was so complete that I was drawn into it and felt not the slightest disgust at my task. I felt that she required me as no one had ever or would ever require me again.

Gradually the character of the contractions changed. They came closer together, were of long duration, some as long as ninety-five seconds, contained multiple peaks that I could feel with my hand against her stomach, and were so regular, fifteen seconds apart, that I stopped looking at my watch and took to counting out the time aloud. Diana gasped, between two of these, "I'm in transition now, I think." She gave me a pleading look, then, as another contraction began, returned to her rapid breathing. At the next break, she said, her eyes meeting mine fully for the first time in hours, "Could you see . . ." She glanced down past her stomach. "If you could tell?"

I understood what she wanted and she had explained to me what I was to look for but I felt the first qualms of inadequacy rising in me as I lifted the sheet from her legs and rested my hand upon one of her damp thighs. "Should I do it now?" I said. She sucked in her breath quickly. "Next one," she spit out the words between breaths. I waited, one hand resting just below her breasts, until I felt the uterus relaxing. Then I slipped my other hand up Diana's taut thigh and timidly explored her vagina. I smiled a little at how often I had done this under different circumstances and what an exciting sensation it had always been. I thought for a moment of Alex. But then I was discovering things unexpected and important. I could feel the rim of the cervix, just as she had described it to me, and past it something simultaneously soft and resistant, something so unfathomable that when my fingertip touched it I drew it back as if I had been stung. I stretched my fingers across the rim and memorized that position, then withdrew my hand.

Diana's eyes were fixed on me as she took breath for another contraction. I held my bloody fingers up in the position I had memorized. Her eyes widened. At the end of the contraction she whispered, "You're sure?"

"Exactly," I said. I didn't know where I was getting my confidence, but I was sure of what my senses told me.

"It's almost there," she said. "About an inch more."

"I think so," I said. "I felt the baby's head."

She smiled. "You did? You felt it?"

"You're doing terrific," I said. "It can't be too much longer."

But it was another hour, and toward the end of it I thought she must expire before my eyes. Her lips were peeling, her eyes were sunken, her expression was one of mindless submission. I made my examinations every ten minutes, but nothing seemed to be happening. She told me, breathlessly, that she experienced with each contraction a powerful urge to bear down, which she knew she was not to do, and so she blew air out in rapid puffs, her eyes nearly closed from exhaustion, her legs trembling beneath my hands. There was no time to speak and in the moments we shared between contractions she gazed at me as if I were miles away. "I'm in another world," she said weakly.

Finally an examination revealed not only the desired expanse of cervix but the baby's head fully crested. "Now," I said. "You can push now." Her eyes came open and she lifted her head to look at me. "What?" she said. "Are you sure?"

"Yes," I said. "Go ahead."

She fell back and I prepared, as well as I could, to receive the baby in my inexperienced hands. Strangely, the contractions stopped. Diana sat up a bit, she appeared to have renewed strength. "Is there room?" she said.

I had pulled the sheet away and stood gazing at the wet oval of the baby's head, surrounded by blood and vaginal tissue stretched so tightly that it was blue. I couldn't tell what would happen, as I didn't know how big the child's head was, but it looked as if another inch would tear the surrounding flesh. "Christ, Diana," I said. "I don't know. I don't think so."

"Can you make a cut with the razor?"

I felt the color leave my face. She had told me of this possibility and had described how it would be done, but I had never thought for a moment that I could do it. As I pondered how to tell her, she was seized with another contraction.

"Go ahead," I said. "Bear down hard. Relax your legs."

She did as I instructed. The baby's head advanced an inch, then dropped back half that distance. When she breathed easily again, I said, "He's not moving much."

"Please," she said, her hand reaching out toward my own. "I don't want to tear. You'll have to do it." Another contraction, stronger than the last. She raised her shoulders from the table, bearing down against it, and when it was past I saw, at the base of the baby's head, that the skin had begun to tear. Diana looked at me, pleading with me, though she was unable to speak. I picked up the razor and made a small cut at the point where the tear had begun. The skin leaped back from the blade and I pulled it away, stunned by what I had done and terrified that I had done it badly. I looked at Diana, who didn't appear to be in more pain than she had been in before. "It's done," I said. A contraction began and she raised herself again, bearing down so hard that her face went from white to pink to red to purple. I saw this change in a second, during which I saw as well that the child's head had advanced considerably. No sooner was the contraction over than another began. I put my hands together near the baby's head and suddenly, in one smooth and graceful motion, he emerged, falling from the womb into my outstretched hands. He was crying and so slippery that I nearly dropped him and fell back on my haunches to catch him to my chest. I heard Diana sigh and drop back on the table. I stood up and raised her son so that she could see him. "A boy," I said.

Her eyes were wide and took him in greedily. "He's perfect," she said. And as I looked down at his blood-soaked limbs, his open mouth, his matted hair and eyelashes, his fingernails, his ears, his inflated nostrils sucking in, for the first time, the damp salt-laden air, I saw that he was perfect and I said, "Yes, yes, he is."

"The lights," Diana said, grimacing at the bright one overhead. The switch was next to me and I pressed it. There was still light in the cabin, for Diana had left one on in the shower. She pulled herself up and reached out for her son. I laid him in her arms, uncertain what to do about the cord. When I touched it I could feel it pulsing, blood coursing through it into the new life. Diana, who did not appear confused by anything, rested the baby in her lap and grasped the cord between her thumb and forefinger. She waited a moment, then took up the razor and cut it, knotting it quickly.

"You're magnificent," I said.

"I'm just glad I read all those books. I would have been screaming if I hadn't." She lay back and held the baby on her stomach, face down. She stroked his back and legs until his curled limbs began to stretch out and he stopped crying. "Christopher," she said softly. "Christopher." I stood watching, aware suddenly of my own exhaustion, which was coupled with a feeling of such overwhelming excitement that I found I hadn't the energy to calm down.

"Could you take him?" Diana said after a while. "The placenta still has to come. I'd like to be alone."

I took the baby and he began to cry. "Try taking your shirt off," Diana suggested. I did so and when I took him from her again he didn't cry but turned his face away and looked toward the light from the shower.

"Can he see?" I asked.

"A little," she said. She was readjusting herself on the table and the expression on her face reminded me of her desire to be alone. "I'll take him out," I said, "to see the moon."

When I stepped out of the cabin I was surprised to find it so bright. There was a full moon and it bled on the water with streaming ribbons of silver. I went to the bow and stood looking out over the lake. The baby was quiet in my arms, his small face turned away from mine so that I couldn't see his expression but could determine that his eyes were open. I felt his even, rapid breathing. The air was so warm, so damp, it was like a caress and I had a sensation of such supreme well-being that I felt myself perfectly frozen in time and space, like the gesture of a statue, or the unbidden recollection of a dream. The person I held in my arms, a novice at breathing, a stranger to light, fresh from a world that was close and full of surging blood, moved his tiny hand against my chest, opening and closing his fist. I smiled and resisted an impulse to hold him up over my head so that he might see the whirling moon, the gleaming stars, the warm, terrible, dark beauty of the universe he was born into.

I thought of Alex, her black hair like the void surrounding me, her skin as cool as the moon, her eyes flashing, not like stars, but with a star's distance, a light that appears ages after its inception.

And then, suddenly, I remembered something I had forgotten and that memory was so powerful I was thrown back in time. I was a child and I lay on the floor burning with fever, my face irritated by the rug beneath my cheek. I heard a footstep, rolled onto my back, and looked up. There she was, bending over me, her arms outstretched, lifting me from the floor and cradling me in her arms, her hair brushing my eyes, her lips cooling my cheeks with a kiss, my beautiful, my adoring mother as I had never recollected her before or since.

The baby let out a sharp cry, as if he felt the need for a sound, then, shocked by his own power, fell silent. He turned his face toward me and I felt his wet mouth against my chest. What a miracle, I thought, too deep to be fathomed, too powerful to be mentioned, that life comes from life, blood from blood, breath from breath. I was a happy witness, bathed in the pearly moonlight, rocked by the even undulations of the water, noticing in the distance the glimmer of light that would grow into a Coast Guard boat; our rescuers on their way. I watched with a feeling of incredulity as the light grew brighter. What would it be like, I wondered, to see strange faces again?

We had plenty of time. I went back to the cabin to tell Diana and found her half asleep. She had wrapped all the sheets together in a bundle and lay on a beach towel on the floor. As I bent over her she reached up, touched her child, touched my cheek, and said, "We're friends for life, now."

"For life," I said. She took the baby and cradled him in her arms so that he could reach her breast, which he nuzzled and sucked with his pale lips, seeming to know what was expected but not sufficiently self-possessed to accomplish it.

"There's a boat coming," I said. "Can I get you anything?"

She glanced down at her crotch. "Some ice," she said, then laughed. "Could you wrap it in a towel? And something to cover myself."

I went to the refrigerator. When I opened the door I saw

that my hands were caked with blood. There was blood on my chest and on my forearms. I washed my hands at the sink and began turning ice from a tray, one cube at a time.

Two hours later we arrived at Beaufort, towed in by the astounded Coast Guard crew, who couldn't stop telling one another the story of how they had found us. Diana's doctor was waiting on the dock, cantankerous, threatening her and her son with disease and imminent death. Alex stood behind him and as I assisted Diana onto a stretcher (she said she could walk but when she tried to stand she paled and clung to me) I was aware of the coldness of Alex's gaze. She climbed onto the boat and nodded at me, then passed me to look into the cabin. She winced at what she saw, and turned to me. "Quite an adventure," she said.

"Beyond my wildest imaginings."

She turned away and went to the rail. Before she jumped to the dock she said, without looking at me, "You have blood on your face."

I touched my cheek self-consciously, then laughed. She didn't look back but walked up to the house behind the doctor, the Coast Guard captain, Diana, and Christopher. I turned my attention to the cabin and began running water into a bucket to wash the blood off the floor.

13

Christopher changed all our lives, but none so drastically as my own. Diana's mothering was ferocious and indolent by turns. She had the best instincts and proceeded without nervousness. Christopher was not much trouble. He nursed, he slept, he gazed upon us. But he was particular and showed a marked preference for my hands. Collie was occupied most of the time, and a good deal of his care fell to me, or, rather, I took it on. I felt the greatest interest in him, and because a touch of my hands was often enough to quiet him, his company was pleasant to me. When he cried I put him across my shoulder and walked about with him. Diana entrusted him to me as she would to no one else.

Collie was delighted with the boy and couldn't have the story of his delivery repeated often enough. She advised Diana on his care, and upon observing how much time he spent in my arms, she sewed up a sling which fit across my shoulders and tied at my waist, in which Christopher could recline comfortably, leaving my hands and arms free. This invention facilitated his care and I began to take him along on my morning walks.

Alex rarely touched the baby. She smiled and complimented Diana upon him but in private she confided that she found him "unformed," and "too helpless." Her opinion neither surprised nor annoyed me. I felt that she resented my affinity for the boy and that he represented something vast to her, some interruption in our intimacy, which she could scarcely tolerate. If I spoke of Christopher she affected boredom or contradicted me; when I held him, she found excuses to leave the room. Something else had changed between us. My passion for Alex was unabated but hers for me seemed to have gained intensity. Our lovemaking was as satisfactory as it had always been and I continued my concentration upon her pleasure, which had, quite naturally, become my pleasure. But I sensed in her response a new seriousness for which I couldn't account. Frequently, as I watched her, the expressions that flickered across her face intrigued me, for she seemed to be on the edge of pain. She turned her face from me but I held her by the hair so that she was forced to look at me. Before and after, but never during orgasms, she opened her eyes and looked into my own. Our intimacy during these moments was so deep it shocked me. I couldn't curb my desire for more. When I think of this now I am devoured by hopelessness and want to call out to her, Alex, Alexandra, how could you have made this stupid decision? How can it be that you can leave me? What else but that which was between us could possibly matter? Your integrity, your self-esteem, take my advice, if you can hear me, and throw them to the wind.

She had always been quarrelsome, and in a superior fashion she deigned to challenge certain of my opinions or to remind me that I must keep a certain distance, that her privacy could be shared but only as it suited her. This quality was one of many that had attracted me to her, though occasionally I felt the desire to shake her and say, "Who do you think you are?" But now our quarrels were more frequent and their subjects often trivial, often concerning my affection for Christopher and Diana.

One morning when Christopher was nearly two months

old, something happened that brought her true condition into the open, though, with my usual lack of insight, I failed to see it until it was thrust upon me.

I had taken Christopher out with me on my morning walk. I had made an effort to keep the front of Banjo's maze open, retaining only the pleasant walks that I knew. The back section, which contained his house, was now as wild as if it had never known any alteration by human hands. This was one of the few times during the day when Christopher was awake and he liked nothing better than to lie in his pouch and watch the tall grasses, sometimes rocked by the rhythmical motion of my arms as I hacked the impeding foliage with a dull but still effective machete. I had tired of this work and Christopher had fallen asleep. After one last walk around the circle I decided to take him in to bed. As we came out on the lawn I heard raised voices coming from the other side of the house. I recognized Diana's deep-voiced vexation and then my heart sank as I heard the shrill reply. I stopped and for a moment thought to slip back into the woods, but my curiosity, and a sense of dread for what might happen if I didn't go, propelled me forward. The voice was Mona's. I would have known it (and somehow expected it) had I been on another planet.

I ran quietly around the house and came out just above the dock. A small motorboat was moored there, too small to have made the trip across the lake. Then I saw the name of the rental company in Covington emblazoned on the prow. So she had driven over and rented it there. On the dock she stood, legs apart, arms moving wildly at her sides, her back, luckily enough, facing me. She was screaming at Diana, who stood some distance away on the lawn, her eyes wide and her upper lip raised on one side, as if she looked upon some disgusting sight, some animal disporting itself grotesquely and tastelessly. Mona said, "It wouldn't surprise me if you bitches had killed him."

Diana laughed.

A figure in black emerged from the other side of the house

and moved quickly toward the two women. Mona recognized her, though she had never seen her, and turned on her with such viciousness that she salivated too heavily and a spray of water accompanied her snarl. "There she is. She's the bitch."

Alex paused in her tracks and looked questioningly at me. Mona followed her gaze and, dumbstruck but determined, lifted her arms as if she intended to enfold me in them.

Then several things happened at once. I noticed that Alex had a knife in each hand. Mona noticed the child sleeping on my side and let out a horrified cry. "Oh my God," she said. Diana waved an arm at Alex as if to impede her progress but she was too late. One of the knives ripped into the board an inch from Mona's shiny leather shoe. The other flew through the air like a flash of light, tore into the fabric of Mona's blouse, into the skin of her shoulder, hung there for a millisecond while blood rushed out to mark the spot, then fell heavily out and landed, blade up, at her feet. She screamed and fell to her knees. Alex cast me a look of cold disdain, turned on her heels, and disappeared behind the house. Diana advanced toward the weeping Mona, a smile of undisguised amusement on her lips.

"She tried to kill me," Mona howled. "She'll pay for this."

I joined Diana and between us we got Mona to her feet and led her, cursing and threatening, up to the house. In the kitchen, when her blouse was removed and the superficial injury, a thin slice in a plump, befreckled, and entirely unappetizing shoulder, was revealed, she dissolved in tears and was unable to say anything coherent. Collie cleaned the wound and muttered over the dangers of having a poor mad creature like Miss Alex exposed to the outside world. Diana and I hid our smiles beneath sighs of agreement.

At last Mona was rearranged and she had dried her too ready tears on a linen napkin. She gave me a wounded look, then glanced at Diana, whose calm beauty made her look, and must have made her feel, a dowdy hysteric. She asked if she might speak to me alone. I gave Christopher to his mother and led my relentless and unwelcome visitor to the library. When I closed the doors she threw herself down in a chair and crossed her legs, ready for battle.

"Why didn't you tell me she was pregnant?" she said. "Don't you think it would have made a difference to me?"

"Who was pregnant?" I said.

"Alex."

"But she wasn't," I said. "The boy is Diana's child."

She looked confused. "Oh," she said, then fell into moody silence.

"How do you happen to know her name?" I inquired.

"Oh, I know everything. The whole pathetic business. I've been frantic trying to reach you. Why didn't you answer my letters?"

"I never received them," I said.

"No. I'm not surprised. It looks as if she has everything under control here." She began fishing about in her purse and came up with a pack of cigarettes, which she held out to me.

"No thanks," I said. "I quit."

"I had to come," she said, lighting up. "Someone has to bring you to your senses."

"I believe I'm in my senses," I said.

She took two quick puffs from her cigarette and spat out the smoke, looking at me reflectively. "When are you coming back?" she said.

I stood looking down at her and I couldn't help but smile, she was so serious on her fool's errand. I tried to think of polite ways in which to give her this information, but as none was forthcoming, I said, "I would rather be dead than go back to that life." As I said this I had the remarkable realization that I really didn't remember that life. Was it possible that I had made love to this absurd woman?

Mona, unfortunately, remembered every detail. "Was it really so bad? Of course, I realize I can't support you in this fashion," she said, sneering at the room.

"Do you think I owe you money?" I said. "I'll gladly reimburse you."

"How can you do this," she said. "Have you no self-respect? Don't you know what your friends think of you? What everyone thinks of you?"

"Why should I give a damn what anyone thinks?" I said. "I want you to get out of here at once and if you don't go I shall carry you down to the dock and throw you in the river."

She laughed.

I longed for one of Alex's knives.

"So you're in paradise," she said. "How much longer do you think your young girl will want you? Hasn't she tired of you already?"

Never had I felt such a desire to hurt a woman. I turned and left the room, slamming the door behind me. I went up to my room and slammed that door, too. Alex was lying on her back on my bed. She opened her eyes, then closed them again. "How could you fuck that pig?" she said flatly.

I leaned against the door. "Mechanically," I said.

She snorted, then pulled herself up to a sitting position. "You make me sick," she said.

I smiled to myself. I decided to let her get to the door before throwing her on the couch. She took a step toward me, then stopped.

"Have you been keeping my mail?" I asked.

"From her? Those drippy letters?"

"You read them?"

"Oh, my darling Claude," she said in a voice so like Mona's it made me laugh. "At night, alone in my bed, I dream of your warm lips crushing my own."

There was the sound of voices downstairs, Mona being escorted, still protesting, to the door. Alex tilted her head, listening. I noticed a few strands of hair curling across her shoulder, pointing to that most vulnerable spot in the throat between the two clavicle bones. I stepped forward quickly, catching her off-guard, and pinned her arms behind her, pressing my mouth against the white skin of her throat, vexed by my strong desire to sink my teeth into that flesh and tear it away. She didn't struggle but dropped her head back so that I might more easily caress her. "Have you tired of me?" I said and as I spoke I opened her blouse and slipped my hand inside. For answer she laughed and wrapped her legs around me. I carried her the few steps to the bed and we fell heavily across it.

When I woke up, Alex was not in the room. I didn't remember falling asleep. We had been talking. I was trying, in my haphazard fashion, to determine if she had intercepted any other mail (though I couldn't think of anyone who would write to me), and then I was awake and she was gone. I sat up and rubbed my eyes. She would probably be annoyed; she hated it when I fell asleep while she was talking. Most people look their age in their sleep and I doubted that I was any different. I imagined how such a sight would disgust her—my mouth slack, snoring perhaps—and how she would turn away. I got to my feet and searched the bed for my pants. I could hear Mona asking if Alex hadn't tired of me yet and I smiled at the recollection it brought. In my fury over this remark I had treated Alex with alternating bursts of violence and solicitousness and she had responded in kind. At one point, when I had pulled her roughly half off the bed so that she landed on her knees, her arms flung out, her hands clinging to the sheets, the pillows, the mattress, I had seen her upper lip curl back over her clenched teeth as she sucked back her escaping breath. No, I thought, she hadn't tired of me.

I dressed and went downstairs. The house was quiet. A glance out the front door told me Mona and her rented boat had gone. I noticed that Diana's boat was gone, too, and I recalled that Christopher was to see his doctor in the afternoon. Alex had doubtless gone with her.

I found Collie in the kitchen drinking coffee and laboring over a page of writing. She smiled at me and I went in. I glanced at her paper and saw her sign her name, beneath a scrawled closing line, "Your loving mama." She folded her sheet in half and slipped it into the stationery box.

"If you're busy?" I said.

"I'm done," she replied. "You want some coffee?"

"I do," I said. "Where is everybody?"

She poured a cup and set it before me. "They all gone to the city in quite a huff, most of it being over you."

"Because of my visitor?" I inquired.

She smiled. "Just what is it you do to these women, Claude? You look harmless but they all ready to kill for you."

"That's not true," I said. "Mona is a sad lonely creature with an unfortunate memory for detail and Alex is just ready to kill, period."

"And Diana?"

"Is Diana angry?"

"She's put out with Alex. She told her if she couldn't treat you no better she deserved to lose you."

This surprised me. "What did Alex say to that?" I asked.

"She said she couldn't lose you if she tried but she was damn well going to try, anyway."

I sat quietly drinking my coffee. I was thinking that if Mona had caused Alex any serious second thoughts about me, I would beat her until I was exhausted. I covered my face with my hands. I had the horrible suspicion that when Diana returned Alex wouldn't be with her. Through my fear I could hear Collie's calm speculation.

"I don't know," she said. "I think Alex been staking too much on you. You're her last-ditch effort. But she just can't bear too much closeness with no one. She gets so tense you can feel it all over the house."

"I know," I said behind my hands.

"And she's not liking that baby, she's jealous of Diana and you. She was so mad the night that child was born she cried herself to sleep on the floor in my room."

I sat up. "She did?"

Collie smiled, cat-like in her terrible deep vision of us all. "You didn't know that, did you?"

I looked away. "I've always known," I said, "that she would leave me. There's my age. And my general uselessness." I paused.

"You thought you had her," she said.

"Yes," I admitted. "I thought so."

"Well, don't listen to me. You may have her yet."

I pushed my coffee away. "I'm going for a walk," I said.

I walked for an hour. Then I sat on the dock and waited. Another hour passed. At last I heard the boat approaching. As it came in sight around the curve in the river my heart stopped. Diana was steering in the cabin, Alex was not on the boat. I stood up and shifted my weight from foot to foot until Diana was near enough to hear me. "Where is she?" I shouted.

She smiled, hushing me with a gesture that indicated the travel bed in which Christopher slept. When she was close enough I jumped onto the prow and threw a rope over a cleat. She came out of the cabin to assist me.

"Where is she?" I said again.

"She'll be back in the morning," she replied. "She had some business to clear up."

"Do you really believe that? What business could she have?"

"Calm down." She touched my arm as she said this, in her most tentative manner, as if touch were painful to her but she would endure it for my sake. "She's bringing the car to Covington and the boat-rental man will bring her out in the morning. She'll be here after breakfast."

"Did you two quarrel?"

Diana turned away and concentrated on tightening a second rope. "Yes," she said.

Nor could I get her to tell me anything more.

14

I slept uneasily that night and rose early in the morning.
Diana and Christopher were still asleep. Collie was pouring
her own first cup of coffee when I joined her. The weather
had changed during the night; it was damp and gusty, the
wind thrusting the sun-baked branches of the trees against
the house so that they sounded like birds scratching to get in.
Collie was quiet, and as I knew she knew what disturbed me,
her company wasn't unpleasant. When I heard Diana moving
upstairs, I slipped out the door and went down to the dock.

There I sat and bedeviled my overtired imagination for
three hours. At last I heard the hum of an outboard motor
and a few moments later Alex placed her booted foot on the
board next to my own. I was weak with anticipation and
found, in spite of the numerous speeches I had prepared, I
was at a loss for words. She spoke briefly to the man who
propelled the little boat away from us, calling out that he
should be careful, for the weather was treacherous. When he
was out of sight she turned to me.

"So," she said. "Here I am." She gave me a guilty look
and tapped one foot nervously.

"You're very nervous," I observed.

"No. I'm not," she said.

I looked down at her foot. "You're tapping your foot."

She stopped her foot and looked away, out over the water, where there was nothing to see.

"Shall we go inside?" I suggested.

"Yes," she said. We turned and walked toward the house.

"What did you do in town?" I asked, controlling my desire to scream this inquiry at the top of my lungs.

"I had some business to clear up," she said.

"Nothing unpleasant, I hope."

"No," she said. "Well, not entirely."

Perhaps, I thought, I was wrong. Perhaps nothing had changed.

The wind blew her hair back from her face, exposing her pale profile. "I love it when it's like this," she said, lifting her chin to indicate the air moving erratically around us.

"I thought maybe we were in for a hurricane," I said. "Did you hear anything about it in town?"

She looked at me absently. "A hurricane? No, there's no hurricane."

We arrived at the steps and she stopped, turning to watch a bird fighting the wind.

"When I was a girl," she said, "and the weather was like this, I used to imagine that I would be a saint."

"A saint?" I veiled my incredulity.

She turned away from the weather and went into the house. "Collie's mother was very religious," she said. "She raised me to think I would be delivered." She laughed. "But I never was."

"How can you be certain?" I said.

She stopped and turned to me, giving me a sad smile as she took my hand in her own and pressed my palm to her cheek. Her skin was warm.

"Alex," I said, "I'm sorry about Mona. I don't know how she found me or what good she thought it would do her."

"Don't be sorry," she said. "Though I'm afraid you will be when you find out how she has affected me."

"I don't understand," I said.

"I wanted to kill her. I was sorry I didn't."

I said nothing.

"Come upstairs." She led the way. "I've got to talk to you."

In my room she sat down on the couch and brushed the nap backward with the palms of her hands. "I think you've guessed that I'm leaving."

I leaned my back against the door frame, feeling a sudden need for some firm support. I thought hysterically of crying out for crutches. "You're going back to the city?"

"Yes," she said. "I've opened my apartment up and I've got my old job back."

"When do you start?"

She looked past me, through the doorway. "Tomorrow."

I closed the door without speaking. Then I took a chair near her. "Have you spoken to Diana about this?"

"No." She grimaced. "I haven't spoken to Diana about anything lately. I think her experiment was a flop."

"What experiment?"

"This place," she said, opening her hands to the air. "And this thing with Christopher. It annoys her that I don't slobber all over him . . ." She paused.

"The way I do," I said.

"Going out with her on that boat that day was the worst thing you ever did."

"I didn't have much choice. Neither did she."

"She knew it. And now you have this wonderful intimacy with her."

"I don't regret the experience, Alex. It was important to me."

"It makes me sick. You two both make me sick."

"I'm sorry for that. She wanted you with her."

"Well, I didn't want to be there. I never did. She never asked me, but if she had I would have told her no. I know you think I'm saying that because I'm jealous. I know that's what you think."

"I don't know what I think."

"I've got to get out of here," she said. She fell back on the couch and fixed me with an impassive stare.

"All right," I said. "Of course, I'll leave, too. Not with you." I paused, confused by my own words. "In a few days . . ." I said.

"There's no need for you to go. Diana won't want you to. She needs you here now."

"And you won't need me there?"

"No," she said softly, her eyes fastened on the ceiling.

"How fortunate for me," I said, "to be passed from hand to hand with such ease. I feel part of some great succession."

"You can suit yourself," she said sharply.

"I know that," I replied. "I've always known that."

An unpleasant silence fell between us. I watched her half-averted face, determined that I would say no more. She sniffed, rubbed her eyes with the heels of her hands, pulled at the tops of her boots, refused to meet my eyes. At last she said, "I know I owe you an explanation and I do plan to give you one." At last she looked at me, blushing deeply. "It's just hard for me to speak of it. I can't talk about sex comfortably."

"Are you shy?" I asked.

"Not shy. I'm humiliated."

"Not by me?"

"I know you don't mean to humiliate me. But you do."

"How can I?" I protested. "Surely my feelings for you are no secret."

She sniffed. "Aren't they?"

"It's you who are secretive."

"I'm not secretive at all," she said sharply. "I'm a simple obsessive person. I have no control over myself."

"Who does?"

"You do," she said.

"I'm just old," I said. "Too old to argue with you."

"I don't believe that."

"Nevertheless, it's true."

"It doesn't matter, anyway," she said. "It's myself I have to live with and it's myself I can't bear."

"Alex, what is going on?"

She laughed. "You can't see it, you haven't noticed?" She held out a trembling hand for my inspection. "Look at this. I don't do this. I've lost control."

"You mean you don't know how you feel?"

She scowled. "I know how I feel well enough. I wish I didn't. Would you like to hear about it?"

I nodded without looking at her. I had never seen her in this mood.

"Good," she said. "I think you should know. It goes like this. I wake up and I feel awful and ashamed. Then I go over whatever we did in bed the last time, and I go over it again and again until I feel sort of dreamy and warm. And then I get up and start prowling around here, waiting for you. My skin is so sensitive if I brush against the railing on the stairs it makes me want to sit down and sigh. When I see you I can hardly make polite conversation. I don't care about anything either of us has to say. I have one thought, will he make love to me soon, will he ask me to go upstairs now, does that look on his face or that gesture mean we should leave now, go now, do it now." These last words caught in her throat and she drew away from me. "I can't think," she continued, "I can't concentrate. The only thing that gives me any pleasure is my knives because I can express my rage with them."

"I don't understand," I began.

"Why I'm angry?"

I nodded again, too weak to speak.

"There's nothing left of me that I can recognize. I don't have any sense, my judgment is shot, my sense of humor is perverse. When I listen to what I'm thinking it makes me sick. When you talk to Diana, when you go off with Christopher, I feel such rage I can hardly catch my breath. I'm lost to myself. I know I was a sensible person. I started this

173

whole thing with you to amuse myself, because I thought you would amuse me. I didn't know it was possible to feel like this." She stopped and bit her lower lip with her upper teeth, as if biting back something she didn't want to say.

"I never meant to make you unhappy," I said.

"Are you kidding?" she snorted. "Do you think I don't know what you want? This is exactly what you want. Nothing could suit you more than to have me wandering around after you like some dog, whimpering for you, any time, anywhere. I may have lost my senses, but I know you've done this to me and you've done it with a vengeance."

"You haven't said anything," I said. "You haven't given me any sign that this was how you felt."

She spoke softly, her anger diminished by her outburst. "I'm giving you a sign now."

I smiled, meeting her eyes. She was smiling too, returning my look affably. I thought her very beautiful and unfathomable. How could she harbor such feelings without my guessing? Hadn't I been near her, day after day, touching her, holding her, concentrating all my energy upon her? How could I have missed her so entirely?

"So you plan to act on this matter," I said.

"I plan to, yes. I'm determined to get away from you."

"When did you begin to feel this way? If you don't mind my asking?"

"It was when you were sick. It was like you were gone and I woke up every night in agony. I would dream about you and wake up excited and know that nothing I could try would work. Nothing could make me feel better. It was physical pain, it drove me mad. I reasoned with myself but it was hopeless. I require you. That was what I found out and I resented it. I can't live like that."

"Why not? I'm sure I require you with equal fervor."

She smiled. "Besides the fact that I'm probably going to be sick, I will miss the way you talk."

Did I smile? I don't believe I did. I looked at her and

could think of nothing to say. Instead, I led her to my bed for what was to be the last time. We both knew it but said nothing and lay on the bed entwining our limbs together. I sought only to get such a grip on her that she might never escape. Alex, never a passive mistress, pulled at my clothing impatiently but, when I tried to assist her, pushed me away. I understood that she had something in mind and for my own part my heart was broken. It wasn't difficult to lie still, which seemed to be what she wanted. Her sharp wet tongue was everywhere upon me; she turned me this way and that, probing me in much the same way that I had often probed her, with helpless abandon and greed, as if I contained some secret she was determined to ferret out. This put me in a state of excitement and she was exacerbated by her success. She played the man and I the woman, and sadly enough, we were quite good at this reversal of roles. But through it all my clear sense of imminent loss possessed me. I pressed her against me with all my strength. I was dimly aware of squeezing her lovely head too tightly between my thighs and thinking, what of it, why not break this cruel and fragile skull. Nor did she struggle but pulled my legs tighter and tighter around her face, her fingers moving across my buttocks. My eyes filled involuntarily with useless tears.

Afterward she lay with her face against my genitals, her tongue flicking out occasionally, lazily, like a lizard on a warm day. I felt myself done for and swore that this detumescence would be my last and that I would never again raise my fatal instrument.

"Thank you," Alex said softly. "That was what I wanted."

I ran my fingers through her hair and spread it over my legs in a web. Without thinking, I asked the question that had long been on my mind. "Did you kill the man who looked like me?"

She sighed. "I never could see the resemblance," she said.

In a few moments she was asleep and I didn't move so as not to disturb her. I'm too old, I told myself, to experience these sensations. I told myself a great deal more but none of it helped. I was as desolated as if I had heard the gates of paradise, grating upon rusty hinges, as they closed at my back.

So here I am at my beginning and I'm sure it's an unsatisfactory turn of events for everyone concerned, especially for you who read this tale. I intend to leave most of the questions I've raised unanswered, for the simple reason that I am not in possession of the answers. I only know what happened. Have I been taken up by something grand or something pitiful, good or evil, for clearly I have been taken up and altered, entirely altered. Before Alex, I was not a man anyone would want to hear about. Now I am extraordinary, though not much wiser.

I don't know whether Alex killed that man, or if there ever was such a man, and really I don't care. I only mention it because it happened, i.e., the suspicion of it happened to me. I can't believe it matters what she was, because of what she is. And she has been good enough, kind enough, to see me in the same way. She treats me (she treated me) as if I was new. And so I was, and so I am.

The past is useless—that is what I've learned. Not just the historical past, which is clearly useless, but our own experience. Because we're never really sure that we know what happened anyway and memory tells us only what should have happened, what we can bear to know. So it's useless to remember, except for pleasure, the way one reads a novel or watches a film, for the sheer fantastic pleasure of it. I can remember Alex's smile the first time I saw her, and I recall the smell of her skin, the taste of her, the involuntary shortness of my breath at the touch of her warm flesh, the inside of her mouth, the pressure of her tongue against my own. And more.

In the future I will have the opportunity to recall her as she is now, asleep in my bed. I watch this sleep and think it must be the sleep of a dictator. Or a murderer. With this innocence, this unshakable certainty about the road to survival, no matter how cruel or senseless, no matter what the cost, with this conviction, she closes her eyes upon the outside without regret.

Is there much sleep like this in the world right now? More than before? Is the mechanism of self-defense this operative in many of us today? Are we really coming out of the darkness of self-sacrifice and guilt and duty into the light of what? Self-knowledge? Is this what it will look like?

God preserve us from sleep like this; it's the death of the spirit, the triumph of the heartless and practical will. But even as I say this I know it is foolishness and that the truth is there is no division, there is no division, the head and the heart are one, have always been, will always be so. We will what we are, and the reverse is also true. If Alex can sleep, then I can let her.

But there is no sleep for me without the certainty that, when I open my eyes again, the vision of her will be gone from me entirely. So I sit here and blink back the temptations of the unconscious, to sleep once and for all.

It is late afternoon. Tonight, who knows what will happen, and tomorrow she will be gone. I find, in spite of my despair, the stirrings of curiosity about my future. Will I ask Diana if she has any use for me (as I have none for myself)? And how will my conversation with her go? I knock at her door, go in, take up Christopher, who lies in his crib contemplating his feet. We sit on the couch. Diana smiles at me. "You look serious," she says.

"Do I? I am. Alex is leaving."

"Yes," she says. "I know."

"So, of course, I'll be going, too. In a few days."

"Do you want to go?"

"I don't care," I say. I rub the patch of saliva Christopher has poured across my pants leg.

"There's work for you here. I need you here. In whatever capacity you choose." Her expression is generous. What is she offering me?

But Diana would never say that. She would say, "There's no need for you to go."

"I can't stay here and live off you. It would hurt my pride."

"Then be in my employ."

"Diana." I say this in a way that indicates my unwillingness to be coerced.

"Banjo is gone. His house is empty. You wouldn't have to stay here."

"No. It would be better if I didn't."

"Though I'll need your help with Christopher."

I hoist him onto my shoulder. He grips my earlobe with his fist and pulls it mercilessly. "He's getting strong," I say.

It could be settled that easily. But, because Alex is doubtless lying about her reasons for leaving, there might be more irony, less agreeableness. We might not be so content to be left to each other. I go in to find Diana standing at the French doors, looking out across the lawn.

"Alex is leaving," I say, alone at the door.

"I know," she says, without turning. "Do you want me to stop her?"

"I don't think you could."

"Don't you?" She turns to me, runs her finger along the dustless table top. "Then you must know more than I."

"I know that she's leaving because of me."

"Oh. Is that what she told you?"

We gaze at each other through the air and between us the vision of Alex fills the space, forcing us apart.

"I thought she was going because of me," she says simply.

"It doesn't matter," I respond. Because it really doesn't matter. When one receives a death sentence, the offense is no longer of interest. "I'll be going in a few days."

"And I'll be left here alone?" She smiles at me.

"With Collie."

"I won't let *you* go." She touches my arm in her tentative way, like a child making sure her friend is still with her. "How could you think for a moment that I would. Without you, now, I would be lost."

In a sense, it's true. Though I'll never know exactly in what sense, Diana and I share a certain responsibility for this loss. So why should we not endure it together.

Or I might be mistaken, Alex might be mistaken. I might sit down and receive only half of her attention. She nurses Christopher and tries to read a music score. "Alex is leaving," I say, alone on the couch.

"I know," she says.

"Of course, I'll be going, too, in a few days." (That much of this conversation seems to be settled.)

To which she responds, "As you wish."

But I think I'm right and that she will use me. To appease my conscience I can turn my savings over to her. In fact, that would be fitting, for, though money means nothing to her, she would accept it as a gesture of my independence. I could have it put in trust for Christopher. Then I could undertake a plan I've toyed with for some time, the revitalization of the maze. I can see myself in Banjo's little house, in twenty years (for I have no doubt my health will hold) sitting at the table over a gas lamp, contemplating my plan, creating a new twist in the path, a cul-de-sac, a window looking into more complications, an unexpected exit. I imagine myself looking up to see Christopher, a young man of excellent integrity and imagination, approaching. Perhaps he carries a violin, or, when he arrives, takes out a worn chess set from the bookshelf. Diana, at forty-five, will be a woman who cannot rest and her son will require my hands, as he did at birth, for deliverance.

And why not? Why shouldn't he have them? What else have I got to do? What could be better? Solitude, obligation, advancing death. I would concentrate on the maze all my energies, so that, at my death, it will be so complex only

Christopher will know the key and the uninitiated will flock to try their luck, only to fail and fail again.

And they will be no more puzzled than I. I make these plans to spite myself. Alex. Alexandra. If I had known what you would cost me I never would have laid a hand on you. I thought I was acquainted with the dreariness of life, with my own dull prospects, but it was nothing to this. Anything would be easier to endure. But this tedium, this lifelessness, this utter sense of loss. What does it matter where I go, what I do, having somehow, through some oversight, lost you. I've lost it all. I'm perfectly free, thanks to you, my sweet love, my cruel intolerant mistress. I hope your integrity is worth this price to you, but the truth is I care nothing for it. How could I believe in such an absurdity? The reasons you gave me were lies, because you are kind and wanted to spare my ego. Of course, of course, I've known it all along. And now I am left to face the remains of my life, in which I will go over your reasons for leaving me again and again until they ring as hollow as they are.

Wasn't there another story I didn't know a thing about? The story of you and Diana. Or the last one about the man who looked like me, whom I failed to resemble in the end, as you hoped I might. Or the story of what you will do back in your apartment, cleaning your boots at the white table, reflecting on your successful destruction of another admirer and the pleasure you plan to take in the next and the next conquest. How easy for you to be so powerful and heartless, the undefeated mistress of how many pathetic hearts.

And one more brief story, of the morning when, dragging myself from the sleep I will have drunk myself into, I hear a sound more hollow still, as my heart grinds to a halt, my name on the lips of some specter. I will greet him on my knees with my arms open wide. And that is the only other embrace I care to contemplate, if you are interested, Alex, if you should ever care to know. At this point, nothing less would do.